P9-EFJ-659

PAY IT FORWARD

CATHERINE RYAN HYDE

— YOUNG READERS EDITION —

Pay It Forward

A Paula Wiseman Book
Simon & Schuster Books for Young Readers
NEW YORK LONDON TORONTO SYDNEY NEW DELHI

If you purchased this book without a cover, you should be aware that this book is stolen property. It was reported as "unsold and destroyed" to the publisher, and neither the author nor the publisher has received any payment for this "stripped book."

SIMON & SCHUSTER BOOKS FOR YOUNG READERS
An imprint of Simon & Schuster Children's Publishing Division
1230 Avenue of the Americas, New York, New York 10020
This book is a work of fiction. Any references to historical events, real people, or real places are used fictitiously. Other names, characters, places, and events are products of the author's imagination, and any resemblance to actual events or places or persons, living or dead, is entirely coincidental.
Text copyright © 1999, 2014 by Catherine Ryan Hyde
This work has been modified from its original version to be suitable for young readers.
Cover illustration copyright © 2014 by Amy June Bates
All rights reserved, including the right of reproduction in whole or in part in any form.
SIMON & SCHUSTER BOOKS FOR YOUNG READERS is a trademark of Simon & Schuster, Inc.
For information about special discounts for bulk purchases, please contact Simon & Schuster Special Sales at 1-866-506-1949 or business@simonandschuster.com.
The Simon & Schuster Speakers Bureau can bring authors to your live event. For more information or to book an event, contact the Simon & Schuster Speakers Bureau at 1-866-248-3049 or visit our website at www.simonspeakers.com.
Also available in a Simon & Schuster Books for Young Readers hardcover edition
Cover design by Laurent Linn
Interior design by Hilary Zarycky
The text for this book is set in Minister.
Manufactured in the United States of America
1014 OFF
First Simon & Schuster Books for Young Readers paperback edition August 2014
4 6 8 10 9 7 5 3
The Library of Congress has cataloged the hardcover edition as follows:
Hyde, Catherine Ryan.
Pay it forward : young readers edition / Catherine Ryan Hyde. — First edition.
pages cm
"A Paula Wiseman Book."
Summary: "Trevor McKinney, a twelve-year-old boy in a small California town, accepts his teacher's challenge to earn extra credit by coming up with a plan to change the world. His idea is simple: do a good deed for three people and instead of asking them to return the favor, ask them to 'pay it forward' to three others who need help"—Provided by publisher.
ISBN 978-1-4814-0941-4 (hardback) — ISBN 978-1-4814-0940-7 (paperback) — ISBN 978-1-4814-0942-1 (eBook)
[1. Kindness—Fiction. 2. Conduct of life—Fiction.] I. Title.
PZ7.H96759Pay 2014
[Fic]—dc23
2013045637

For Vance

A NOTE ABOUT THE YOUNG READERS EDITION BY CATHERINE RYAN HYDE

The book you are holding in your hands has become historical fiction. It's set in the 1990s, when Clinton was first running for president. When newspapers were still the dominant media outlet, and no one had a cell phone.

I imagine that will be an interesting experience for readers of this edition, most of whom had not yet been born.

But it wasn't historical fiction when I wrote it. When I drafted the original edition of *Pay It Forward*, it *was* the 1990s. In fact, the idea for the book was first planted in my head nearly twenty years before that.

Here's how it all began.

It was 1978. I was driving my car, an aging, poorly maintained Datsun (translation for younger people: Nissan) in a bad neighborhood late at night.

I was alone.

It was my own fault that my car was in such miserable condition. I was young in 1978. And I had this theory when I was young. I thought it was cheaper to just drive your car and *not* take it to the mechanic. People laugh when I say that, but it made perfect sense to me at the time. Mechanics cost money, right? Therefore, if you don't go to them, you save money. *Right?* It's thinking reserved for the new driver, and it's one of those theories that works fairly well until the day it doesn't anymore.

This was that day.

I reached the stop sign at the end of the freeway ramp. I put my foot on the brake, and the engine stalled. That might sound unusual to you, but the engine always stalled when I took my foot off the gas. It's what happens when you never take your car to the mechanic.

I reached for the ignition to start it up again, and all the electricity in my car suddenly died. Headlights, dash lights . . . out. Now I was in a bad neighborhood late at night *in the dark*.

Then I noticed a curl of smoke.

Whether or not you've experienced this yourself (and I hope you never have to), you probably know that when you're in a bad neighborhood late at night, you feel a powerful incentive to stay in your car with the doors locked. Until the car fills up with smoke. This might very well be the textbook definition of being "between a rock and a hard place."

I jumped out. Into the bad neighborhood. Alone.

Or so I thought.

I looked up to see two men, two total strangers, running in my direction. Very fast. One of them was carrying a blanket.

Many thoughts danced in my head. I think the first was, *I never made out a will.* Then I realized it didn't matter, because I had nothing to leave to anybody anyway. Except the car. Which was on fire.

Probably other thoughts danced around in there as well. I can tell you one thought I'm sure did not dance: rescue. The crazy idea that these men might be coming to my rescue was, unfortunately, nowhere on the list.

One of the men pushed past me and popped the hood of my car from the inside. The other, the man with the blanket, opened the hood, leaned his entire upper body into my flaming engine compartment, and put the fire out using only the blanket and his bare hands.

I just want to pause here, briefly, for emphasis.

His bare hands. *My* flaming engine compartment. Isn't that a fascinating combination between total strangers? I thought so too.

Right around the time they got the fire out, the fire department showed up. And I have no idea who called them. When speaking to groups of young students, as I often have, they like to guess that someone had a cell phone and I didn't notice. No. Not in 1978. No one had a cell phone. This was back when we had emergency call boxes on the highway. (I guess we still do, but we ignore them, because we all have cell phones.) Apparently, someone going by on the freeway behind us had seen the trouble I was in and stopped to call the fire department.

Now, I certainly would call the fire department for a stranger. I hope most of us would. For anyone. But would I lean my upper body into someone's flaming engine compartment and put out the fire with my bare hands?

That's a big question.

By the time the firefighters arrived, there wasn't much left for them to do. The fire was already out. So they just helped us push my car over to the side of the road. They showed me how the fire started. (Not interesting.) And they explained what would have happened if it hadn't been put out. (Not happy, but interesting.)

You see, the fire was burning along the throttle line. And would soon have made its way back to the gas tank.

That's when I realized: These two men may have saved more than just my car. They may have saved my life. And they may have put their own lives at risk to do so.

I turned around to thank them, and discovered that they had already packed up and driven away. In the confusion of talking to the fire department, they'd left. And I hadn't noticed. This had been the biggest favor I'd ever received, and from total strangers. And I hadn't even said thank you.

So what do you do with a favor that big if you can't pay it back? I think you know. If you don't, just keep reading beyond this introduction.

I've had many people ask me, in response to that story, "So, you're saying that if those two men hadn't stopped that night, the whole 'pay it forward' thing never would have happened?" And I say, "I'll take it a step further than that. *If they hadn't left without saying good-bye*, there never would have been a *Pay it Forward* novel." And if there hadn't been the novel, there wouldn't have been two dozen language translations of it around the world, the movie, the foundation, the real-life global movement. If those two strangers had stayed around to absorb my gratitude, I might simply have gotten their names and sent them a holiday card every year for the rest of our natural lives. And that might have felt like enough.

But they left.

Amazingly, I was able to get the car fixed. And then I went back to driving the freeways for my business. But something had changed.

Me.

Suddenly, I had one eye on the side of the road, looking for someone broken down or otherwise in trouble. And I knew that when I saw such a person, I would stop. And of course I did stop. Even though I never had before.

That act of kindness changed me.

And because it did, I began watching to see if other acts of kindness changed other people. And, almost invariably, I saw that they did. I observed small acts of kindness changing people in small ways. And I felt I'd already proved that a big enough act of kindness can alter the course of a person's life entirely. But, big or small, I've still yet to see acts of kindness fail.

Prologue

Maybe someday I'll have kids of my own. I hope so. If I do, they'll probably ask what part I played in the movement that changed the world. And because I'm not the person I once was, I'll tell them the truth. My part was nothing. I did nothing. I was just the guy in the corner taking notes.

My name is Chris Chandler, and I'm an investigative reporter. Or at least I was. Until I found out that actions have consequences and not everything is under my control. Until I found out that I couldn't change the world at all, but a seemingly ordinary twelve-year-old boy could change the world completely—for the better, and forever—working with nothing but his own altruism, one good idea, and a couple of years. And a big sacrifice.

And a splash of publicity. That's where I came in. I can tell you how it all started.

1

It started with a teacher who moved to Atascadero, California, to teach social studies to junior high school students. A teacher nobody knew very well, because they couldn't get past his face. Because it was hard to look at his face.

It started with a boy who didn't seem all that remarkable on the outside but who could see past his teacher's face.

It started with an assignment that this teacher had given out a hundred times before, with no startling results. But that assignment in the hands of that boy caused a seed to be planted, and after that, nothing in the world would ever be the same. Nor would anybody want it to be.

And I can tell you what it became. In fact, I'll tell you a story that will help you understand how big it grew.

About a week ago my car stalled in a busy intersection, and it wouldn't start again no matter how many times I tried. It was rush hour, and I thought I was in a hurry. I thought I had something important to do, and it couldn't wait. So I was standing in the middle of the intersection looking under the hood, which was a little silly, because I can't fix cars. What did I think I would see?

I'd been expecting this. It was an old car. It was as good as gone.

A man came up behind me, a stranger.

"Let's get it off to the side of the road," he said. "Here. I'll help you push." When we got it—and ourselves—to safety, he handed me the keys to his car. A nice silver Acura, barely two years old. "You can have mine," he said. "We'll trade."

He didn't give me the car as a loan. He gave it to me as a gift. He took my address, so he could send me the title. And he did send the title; it just arrived today.

A great deal of generosity has come into my life lately, the note said, *so I felt I could take your old car and use it as a trade-in. I can well afford something new, so why not give as good as I've received?*

That's what kind of world it's become. No, actually, it's more. It's become even more. It's not just the kind of world in which a total stranger will give me his car as a gift. It's the kind of world in which the day I received that gift was not dramatically different from all other days. Such generosity has become the way of things. It's become commonplace.

So this much I understand well enough to relate: It started as an extra-credit assignment for a social studies class and turned into a world where no one goes hungry, no one is cold, no one is without a job or a ride or a loan.

And yet at first people needed to know more. Somehow it was not enough that a boy barely in his teens was able to change the world. Somehow it had to be known why the world could change at just that moment, why it could not have changed a moment sooner, what Trevor brought to that moment, and why it was the very thing that moment required.

And that, unfortunately, is the part I can't explain.

I was there. Every step of the way, I was there. But I was a different person then. I was looking in all the wrong places. I thought it was just a story, and the story was all that mattered. I cared about Trevor, and I cared about my work, but I didn't know what my work could really mean until it was over. I wanted to make lots of money. I did make lots of money. I gave it all away.

I don't know who I was then, but I know who I am now.

Trevor changed me, too.

I thought Reuben would have the answers. Reuben St. Clair, the teacher who started it all. He was closer to Trevor than anybody except maybe

Trevor's mother, Arlene. And Reuben was looking in all the right places, I think. And I believe he was paying attention.

So, after the fact, when it was my job to write books about the movement, I asked Reuben two important questions.

"What was it about Trevor that made him different?" I asked.

Reuben thought carefully and then said, "The thing about Trevor was that he was just like everybody else, except for the part of him that wasn't."

I didn't even ask what part that was. I'm learning.

Then I asked, "When you first handed out that now-famous assignment, did you think that one of your students would actually change the world?"

And Reuben replied, "No, I thought they all would. But perhaps in smaller ways."

People gradually stopped needing to know why. We adjust quickly to change, even as we rant and rail and swear we never will. And everybody likes a change if it's a change for the better. And no one likes to dwell on the past if the past is ugly and everything is finally going well.

The most important thing I can add from my own observations is this: Knowing it started from unremarkable circumstances should be a comfort to us all. Because it proves that you don't need much to change the entire world for the better. You can start with the most ordinary ingredients. You can start with the world you've got.

CHAPTER ONE

Reuben

January 1992

The woman smiled so politely that he felt offended.

"Let me tell Principal Morgan that you're here, Mr. St. Clair. She'll want to talk with you." She walked two steps, turned back. "She likes to talk to everyone, I mean. Any new teacher."

"Of course."

He should have been used to this by now.

More than three minutes later she emerged from the principal's office, smiling too widely. Too openly. People always display far too much acceptance, he'd noticed, when they are having trouble mustering any for real.

"Go right on in, Mr. St. Clair. She'll see you."

"Thank you."

The principal appeared to be about ten years older than Reuben, with a great deal of dark hair, worn up, a Caucasian, and attractive.

"We are so pleased to meet you face-to-face, Mr. St. Clair." Then she flushed, as if the mention of the word "face" had been an unforgivable error.

"Please call me Reuben."

"Reuben, yes. And I'm Anne."

She met him with a steady, head-on gaze and at no time appeared startled. So she had been verbally prepared by her assistant. And somehow the only thing worse than an unprepared reaction was the obviously rehearsed absence of one.

He hated these moments so.

She motioned toward a chair, and he sat.

"I'm not quite what you were expecting, am I, Anne?"

"In what respect?"

"Please don't do this. You must appreciate how many times I've replayed this same scene. I can't bear to talk around an obvious issue."

She tried to establish eye contact, as one normally would when addressing a coworker in conversation, but she could not make it stick. "You know this has nothing to do with your being African American," she said.

"Oh, yes," he said. "I do know that. I know exactly what it's about."

"If you think your position is in any jeopardy, Reuben, you're worrying for nothing."

"Do you really have this little talk with everyone?"

"Of course I do."

"Before they even address their first class?"

Pause. "Not necessarily. I just thought we might discuss the subject of . . . initial adjustment."

"You worry that my appearance will alarm the students."

"What has your experience been with that in the past?"

"The students are always easy, Anne. This is the difficult moment. Always."

"I understand."

"With all respect, I'm not sure you do," he said. Out loud.

At his former school, in Cincinnati, Reuben had a friend named Louis Tartaglia. Lou had a special way of addressing an unfamiliar class. He would enter, on that first morning, with a yardstick in his hand. Walk right into the flap and fray. They like to test a teacher, you see, at first. He would ask for silence, which he never received on the first request. After counting to three, he would bring this yardstick up over his head and smack it down on the desktop in such a way that it would break in two. The free half would fly up into the air behind him, hit the blackboard, and clatter to the floor. Then, in the audible silence to follow, he would say, simply, "Thank you." And he'd have no trouble with the class after that.

Reuben warned him that someday a piece would fly in the wrong direction and hit a student, causing a world of problems, but it had always worked as planned, so far as he knew.

"It boils down to unpredictability," Lou explained. "Once they see you as unpredictable, you hold the cards."

Then he asked what Reuben did to quiet an unfamiliar and unruly class, and Reuben replied that he had never experienced the problem; he had never been greeted by anything but stony silence and was never assumed to be predictable.

"Oh. Right," Lou said, as if he should have known better.

And he should have.

Reuben stood before them, for the first time, both grateful for and resentful of their silence. Outside the windows on his right was California, a place he'd never been before. The trees were different; the sky did not say winter as it had when he'd started the long drive from Cincinnati. He wouldn't say from home, because it was not his home, not really. And neither was this. And he'd grown tired of feeling like a stranger.

He performed a quick head count, seats per row, number of rows. "Since I can see you're all here," he said, "we will dispense with the roll call."

It seemed to break a spell, that he spoke, and the students shifted a bit, made eye contact with one another. Whispered across aisles. Neither better nor worse than usual. He turned away to write his name on the board. *Mr. St. Clair.* Also wrote it out underneath, *Saint Clair*, as an aid to pronunciation. Then he paused before turning back, so they would have time to finish reading his name.

In his mind, his plan, he thought he'd start right off with the assignment. But it caved from under him, like skidding down the side of a sand dune. He was not Lou, and sometimes people needed to know him first. Sometimes he was startling enough on his own, before his ideas even showed themselves.

"Maybe we should spend this first day," he said, "just talking. Since you don't know me at all. We can start by talking about appearances. How we feel about people because of how they look. There are no rules. You can say anything you want."

Apparently, they did not believe him yet, because they said the same things they might have with their parents looking on. To his disappointment.

Then, in what he supposed was an attempt at humor, a boy in the back row asked if he was a pirate.

"No," he said. "I'm not. I'm a teacher."

"I thought only pirates wore eye patches."

"People who have lost eyes wear eye patches. Whether they are pirates or not is beside the point."

The class filed out, to his relief, and he looked up to see a boy standing in front of his desk. A thin white boy, but very dark haired, possibly part Hispanic, who said, "Hi."

"Hello."

"What happened to your face?"

Reuben smiled, which was rare for him, being self-conscious about the lopsided effect. He pulled a chair around so the boy could sit facing him and motioned for him to sit, which he did without hesitation. "What's your name?"

"Trevor."

"Trevor what?"

"McKinney. Did I hurt your feelings?"

"No, Trevor. You didn't."

"My mom says I shouldn't ask people things like that, because it might hurt their feelings. She says you should act like you didn't notice."

"Well, what your mom doesn't know, Trevor, because she's never been in my shoes, is that if you act like you didn't notice, I still know that you did. And then it feels strange that we can't talk about it when we're both thinking about it. Know what I mean?"

"I think so. So, what happened?"

"I was injured in a war."

"Vietnam?"

"That's right."

"My daddy was in Vietnam. He says it's a nightmare."

"I would tend to agree. Even though I was there for only seven weeks."

"My daddy was there two years."

"Was he injured?"

"Maybe a little. I think he has a sore knee."

"I was supposed to stay two years, but I got hurt so badly that I had to come home. So, in a way, I was lucky that I didn't have to stay, and in a way, your daddy was lucky because he didn't get hurt that badly. If you know what I mean." The boy didn't look too sure that he did. "Maybe someday I'll meet your dad. Maybe on parents' night."

"I don't think so. We don't know where he is. What's under the eye patch?"

"Nothing."

"How can it be nothing?"

"It's like nothing was ever there. Do you want to see?"

"You bet."

Reuben took off the patch.

No one seemed to know quite what he meant by "nothing" until they saw it. No one seemed prepared for the shock of "nothing" where there would be an eye on everyone else they had ever met. The boy's head rocked back a little, then he nodded. Kids were easier. Reuben replaced the patch.

"Sorry about your face. But, you know, it's only just that one side. The other side looks real good."

"Thank you, Trevor. I think you are the first person to offer me that compliment."

"Well, see ya."

"Good-bye, Trevor."

Reuben moved to the window and looked out over the front lawn. Watched students clump and talk and run on the grass, until Trevor appeared, trotting down the front steps.

It was ingrained in Reuben to defend this moment, and he could not have returned to his desk if he'd tried. He needed to know if Trevor would run up to the other boys to flaunt his new knowledge. To collect on any bets or tell any tales, which Reuben would not hear, only imagine from his second-floor perch, his face flushing under the imagined words. But Trevor trotted past the boys without so much as a glance, stopping to speak to no one.

It was almost time for Reuben's second class to arrive. So he had to get started, preparing himself to do it all over again.

From *The Other Faces Behind the Movement* by Chris Chandler

Reuben

There is nothing monstrous or grotesque about my face. I get to state this with a certain objectivity, being perhaps the only one capable of such. I am the only one used to seeing it, because I am the only one who dares, with the help of a shaving mirror, to openly stare.

I have undergone eleven operations, all in all, to repair what was, at one time, unsightly damage. The area that was my left eye, and the lost bone and muscle under cheek and brow, have been neatly covered with skin removed from my thigh. I have endured numerous skin grafts and plastic surgeries. Only a few of these were necessary for health or function. Most were intended to make me an easier individual to meet. The final result is a smooth, complete absence of an eye, as if one had never existed; a great loss of muscle and mass in cheek and neck; and obvious nerve damage to the left corner of my mouth. It is dead, so to speak, and droops. But after many years of speech therapy, my speech is fairly easily understood.

So, in a sense, it is not what people see in my face that disturbs them, but rather what they expect to see and do not.

I also have minimal use of my left arm, which is foreshortened and thin from lack of use, and I am deaf in one ear. My guess is that people rarely notice this until I've been around awhile, because my face tends to steal the show.

I have worked in schools, lounged in staff rooms, where a Band-Aid draws comment and requires explanation. "Richie, what did you do to your

16

hand?" A cast on an arm becomes a story told for six weeks, multiplied by the number of employees. "Well, I was on a ladder, see, preparing to clean my storm drains...."

So it seems odd to me that no one will ask. If they suddenly did, and I were forced to repeat the story, I might decide I liked things better before. But it's not so much *that* they don't ask, but *why* they don't ask, as if I am an unspeakable tragedy, as new and shocking to myself as to them.

From *The Diary of Trevor*

I like the new teacher. I don't know what the deal is with the other kids in my class. Even Joe, who's my friend. They all just stared at him like he was from outer space. At least Joe didn't laugh when Mr. St. Clair wasn't looking.

And the weird thing is, I don't think most of it was his face. I mean, it was. At first. But then he started talking, and you could sort of feel that almost everybody got used to it. A little.

But then he wrote that assignment on the board. He wrote it in really big capital letters, like the blackboard was yelling at us.

THINK OF AN IDEA FOR WORLD CHANGE AND PUT IT INTO ACTION

Man, was it ever quiet in that room.

Finally, Jamie, this girl who's usually really shy, said, "Um. What is that?"

Mr. St. Clair said, "It's an assignment. For extra credit."

More silence.

This guy named Jack, who's much cooler than me and has lots more friends, said, "We're supposed to change the world for social studies class? Isn't that a little . . . hard?"

"You're supposed to think of an idea that might change the world and set it in motion. Whether or not the world actually changes is not part of the assignment."

Then Arnie, who always likes trouble, said, "That's still the hardest assignment anybody ever gave us. We're a bunch of kids. What do you want from us?"

"I want you to think," Mr. St. Clair said. "The first word in this assignment is 'think.' So far you're arguing. Not thinking. That said, if it feels like too much, bear in mind it's for extra credit. It's not required."

But I already totally knew I was going to do it.

I looked around at all the kids in my class. I had to look over one shoulder at a time, because I always sit in the front row. Everybody was just staring at that sentence on the board. Some of the kids looked like they were concentrating, but frowning. And then two of the guys looked away and started whispering to each other, like something was funny.

I looked at my friend Joe, but he just looked totally confused.

I wondered if I was the only one who was going to give the assignment a try. And, if so, why.

CHAPTER TWO

Arlene

Ricky never exactly came home, not like she thought he would, but the truck did. Only not like she thought it would. It had been rolled a few times; all in all, it looked worse than she felt. Only it ran. Well, it idled. It's one thing to start up and run, quite another to actually get somewhere.

Much as she resented that Ford extra cab for imitating her own current condition, she could have forgiven it that. Potentially, she could. It was the way it kept her awake at night. Especially now, when she'd taken a second job, at the Laser Lounge, to keep up the payments. And since it was the truck's fault that she didn't get to bed until three, it at least could have let her sleep. Surely that would not have been asking too much.

Yet there she was again at the window, double-checking the way moonlight slid off the vehicle's spooky shape. The way its silvery reflection broke where the paint broke. Only Ricky could mess up a truck that bad and walk away. At least, it would stand to reason that he had walked away, seeing that the truck was found and Ricky was not.

Dragged off by coyotes? Stop, Arlene, just get ahold of yourself.

Unless, of course, he limped away, not sauntered off, maybe dragged himself to a hospital, maybe got out okay, maybe died, far from anything to tie him to a Ford extra cab, far from any ties to hometown news.

So there could be a grave somewhere, but how would Arlene know? And even if she did, she could not know which one or where. Even if she bought flowers for Ricky out of her tip money, she and her boy, Trevor, would never know where to put them.

Flowers can be a bad thing, a bad thought, if you don't even know where to lay them down. Just stop, Arlene. Just go back to bed.

And she did, but she fell victim to a dream in which Ricky had been living just outside the town for months and months and never bothered to contact her with his whereabouts.

Which made her cross to the window again to blame the darn truck for keeping her awake.

From *The Diary of Trevor*

Sometimes I think my father never went to Vietnam. I don't even know why I think that. I just do.

Joe's father went to Vietnam, and he tells stories. And you can tell, just by the stories, that he really did go.

I think my father maybe just says things sometimes that he thinks will make people proud of him or feel sorry for him.

My mom feels sorry for him because he went to Vietnam. She says no wonder he has problems. So I don't tell her that I think maybe he never did.

Mr. St. Clair is so cool. I don't care what Arnie says. I think he's great, and I'm gonna do such a great job on that assignment, Mr. St. Clair won't even be able to believe it.

CHAPTER THREE

Jerry

He didn't know if it was nine o'clock yet, but it seemed like it must be. Forty-eight people were gathered on the corner, not counting himself.

A boy, twelve, thirteen years old, rode up on a bike, an old beach cruiser. Jerry was surprised that there weren't more kids waiting, because kids like free money. Along with everybody else. But the kid didn't act like he'd come to wait.

The kid looked at the crowd. The crowd looked at him. Maybe because he was the only one so far who didn't keep his eyes down on the pavement. The kid's eyes scanned around like he was counting. His forehead all furrowed down into a frown. Then he said, "Holy cow. Are you all here for the ad?"

He said it in a kind of official way, and some heads came up. Listening to him, sort of. Thinking he might know something. A few people nodded.

"Holy cow." He said it again. Shook his head. "I only wanted one guy."

Jerry walked up to the kid. Nice. Humble, not like to scare him. Said, "You did that ad?"

"Yeah, I did."

And almost everybody left. Whether that meant they thought there was no money or that they wouldn't take it from a kid, Jerry didn't know.

The kid just stood there awhile. Kind of relieved, Jerry thought, because now there were only ten or eleven left. A little more manageable crowd.

Jerry asked, "So, *is* it a joke?"

"No, it's for real. I got a paper route, and I make thirty-five dollars a week, and I want to give it to somebody. Who'll, like, get a job and not need it after a while. Just to get 'em started, you know? Like food and something better to wear and some bus fare. Or whatever."

And somebody behind Jerry, some voice over his shoulder, said, "Yeah, but which somebody?"

Yeah. That was the problem.

The kid thought this over for a bit. Then he said he had some paper in his book bag, and he asked everybody to write out why they thought it should be them.

And when he said that, six people left.

Kid said, "I wonder what happened to them."

And the lady with no front teeth, she said, "What makes you think everybody can write?"

It was clear from the look on the kid's face that he never would have thought of that.

Why I Think I Deserve the Money,
by Jerry Busconi

Well, for starters, I will not say I deserve it better than anybody. Because, who is to say?

I am not a perfect person, and maybe somebody else will say they are. And you are a smart kid. I bet you are. And you will know they are handing you a line. I am being honest.

Me, I have problems sometimes. This is my own fault. Nobody else's. I lost some stuff because of my problems. A car, even though it was not a very good one. And my apartment. And then I went to jail, and they did not hold my job for when I got out.

But I got lots of things I can do. I got skills. I have worked in wrecking yards, and in body shops, and I have even worked as a mechanic. I am a good mechanic. It's not that I'm not. But, used to, you could go in kind of scruffy and dirty. For a mechanic's job, no one would mind.

But now times is hard, and guys show up for the same job. Dressed good, and some even got a state license. So they say, fill out this form. Which I can do. Cause as you see, I can read and write pretty good. But then they say, put down your number. We'll call you if you get the job.

But the dumpster where I been staying ain't got a phone. So I say, I'm just getting settled in. And they say, put your address, then. We'll send you a postcard.

And they know then. That you are on the street. And I guess they figure you got problems, stuff they don't know nothing about.

And, well, I guess I do. Like I said.

But if I had a chance at a job now, I would not mess it up like I have done before. It would be different this time.

Anyway, if you go with me, you won't be sorry. I guess that's all I got to say.

Also, thank you. I never knowed no kid who gave money away. I had a job at your age, and I spent the money on me. You must be a good kid.

I guess that's all now. Thanks for your time.

When Jerry looked up, everybody else except the kid had gone.

CHAPTER FOUR

Arlene

It was not even seven o'clock. Someone was shaking her shoulder, and without being exactly conscious, she knew by instinct that it was her boy.

"Momma? Are you awake?"

"Yeah."

"Can Jerry come in and take a shower?"

She blinked and squinted at the clock. She had another half an hour to sleep. Nothing should have been happening now. A dream maybe, but that's it. "Who's Jerry?"

"My friend."

She hadn't known Trevor to have any friends named Jerry, and now she had forgotten the original request.

"Use your own judgment. I'll be up in a half hour." She folded a pillow around her head, and that was the last thing she remembered until the alarm clock went off and she threw the pillow at it.

A few minutes later, as she set a bowl of hot cereal in front of the boy, a total stranger popped out of the hall and into the kitchen. She was all set to scream but felt too embarrassed to follow through, maybe because, out of the three of them, she was the only one who seemed the least bit surprised.

She figured the man to be in his forties, at least, short, clean shaven, with a receding hairline, and he was wearing brand-new blue jeans and a stiff-looking denim shirt.

"What the—who are you?"

He didn't answer fast enough, so Trevor said, "It's Jerry, Mom. Remember you said he could come in and take a shower?"

"I said that?"

"Yeah."

"When did I say that?"

"Right before you woke up."

Meanwhile, Jerry had said nothing in his own defense or otherwise, but apparently, he was a smart enough man to know when and where he was not wanted, because he began to creep sideways toward the door. "Thank you kindly, ma'am," he said with his hand on the knob, and Trevor asked him, of all the darn things for a kid to say, if he needed money for the bus. The man held out a handful of change. Held it out like war medals or rubies, something a darn sight more important than quarters and dimes, that's for sure. "I saved it, see? From my clothes money."

And Trevor said, "I hope you get the job." And then after the door had closed behind him, Trevor looked up at Arlene like nothing at all had just happened and said, "You know your mouth's hanging open?"

But when he saw the look on her face, he hunkered down over his hot cereal and concentrated on stirring in the sugar.

"Trevor, who the heck was that?"

"I told you. Jerry."

"Who the heck is Jerry?"

"My friend."

"I did not say he could come in here and take a shower."

"Yeah, you did. You said I should use my own judgment."

She had no memory of saying this, but it rang true, in that it was what she would have said if she was really just trying to stay asleep. Unless the boy was smart enough to know that's what she would have said. But it was too early in the morning to sort between things that had happened and those that maybe had, so she said only this: "If your judgment is to let a strange man into our bathroom to shower, then I do believe your judgment needs a tune-up."

He tried to argue again that the man was not a stranger, but rather his friend Jerry, but Arlene was not having any of it. She told him only to eat up and get on to school, and that she did not want to see Jerry in the house anymore, ever, not under any circumstances, no way, José.

The minute Trevor was out the door, she regretted having forgotten to ask why he offered Jerry money for the bus.

She went straight to the bathroom, which the man had left surprisingly neat, and commenced to sterilize every exposed surface.

Maybe three days later, maybe four, Arlene arrived home after working at the Laser Lounge until three a.m. to discover someone in the driveway tinkering with a light on the wrecked truck. And the fact that she pulled up in front of her own house did not seem to discourage him from his work.

She had been afraid of this, being gone as much as she was. Every time someone came to buy parts off the truck and then drove away without buying something, she was half afraid they would come back in the night and take what they wanted. And now look.

With a big, deep breath, she kicked the back door open directly onto the driveway, where the man crouched, working by the light of a metal lamp clipped to the bumper. And plugged in somewhere in her own garage. Which made her madder somehow—that some low-life thief would use her electricity to see better while robbing her blind.

He jumped up and turned to face her in the dark. "It's only me," he said.

"Only you who?"

"Jerry."

Oh, Arlene thought. *Jerry. Great.* "What're you takin' off my truck?"

"Everything, ma'am. I been stacking parts in the garage. Trevor told me you were parting out. You can get a lot more money that way. Did you know that? You got to give a price break if the people have to pull those parts on their own."

"So you're just trying to help out," she said, in tone that made it clear she didn't think so.

"Yes, ma'am."

"At three o'clock in the morning."

"Yes, ma'am. I got me a job now during the day, at the Quicky Lube and Tune a few miles down on the Camino. So if I'm going to help out, it's got to be at night."

She couldn't see his face as well as she'd have liked, dark as it was, but his voice sounded pretty matter-of-fact, and the whole incident was beginning to get under her skin. Picking up his little work light, she walked to the garage to see for herself. He had parts stacked all neat in there, with a door and a bumper and seats. And he had things labeled with something like a grease pencil: *Driver's Side. Front. Rear.*

She stepped out again and shone the light straight at him. He threw a hand up to shield his eyes.

"Did I ask you to help?"

"No, ma'am. But it's something I'm good at. I used to work at a wrecking yard. And the boy's helped me out a lot."

"Trevor been giving you money?"

"Yes, ma'am. Just to help me get on my feet. You know, to get cleaned up enough to get a job again. Like that."

32

"And now you got a job, you gonna pay him that money back?"

"No, ma'am. I'm not allowed to. I have to pay it forward."

"'Pay it forward'? What the heck does that mean?"

He seemed surprised that she was not familiar with the term. And meanwhile, it had become something like a normal conversation, with Arlene not entirely having the upper hand, and the fact that she couldn't get mad at him made her even madder.

"You don't know about that? You oughta talk to him. I'm surprised he didn't tell you about it. Something he's working on for social studies class. He could explain it better, though. You know, if you got ten bucks to rent a hoist, I'll pull that engine and put it up on blocks and tarp it. Save you a bundle."

"No offense to you personally, but I told Trevor I did not want you around the house."

"I thought you told him you didn't want me *in* the house."

"What's the difference?"

"Well. The difference is, one way I'm in the house. And the other way I'm out of it."

"Excuse me. I think I better go have a talk with my boy."

33

But Trevor was so sleepy, all he could say was, "Hi, Momma," and "Is everything okay?" and when she told him Jerry was out in the driveway taking the truck apart, he said, "That's good."

And she couldn't be upset with him. He was just like his father in that respect.

Because it is always so much easier to blow off steam to a stranger, Arlene went down to Trevor's school to have a talk with this Mr. St. Clair. She went to the office first thing, before class started in the morning, hoping she would not even run into Trevor and that he would never have to know she'd been there. The office lady told her to go right up.

She got halfway through the door into his classroom, stopped, and misplaced all that good steam she had built up. Because she had never seen a man with only half a face. It's one of those things. Takes a minute to adjust to. And she knew if she took even one minute more, he would notice that she had noticed his unfortunate scarring, which would be just plain rude. This whole scene had all gone very smoothly in her mind on the way to school, where she had been angry, well spoken, and really quite good.

34

She moved through the room toward his desk. He was still waiting for something to be said.

"What's 'paying forward'?"

"Excuse me?"

"That expression. 'Paying forward.' What does it mean?"

"I give up. What does it mean?"

"That's what you are supposed to tell me."

"I would love to, madam, if I knew. If you don't mind my asking, who are you?"

"Oh, did I forget to say that? Excuse me. Arlene McKinney." She reached her hand out, and he shook it. Trying not to look at his face, she noticed that his left arm was deformed somehow, the wrong size, which gave her the shivers for just a second. "My boy is in your social studies class. Trevor."

Something came onto his face then, a positive recognition, which, being connected in some way to her boy, made her like this man better. "Trevor, yes. I like Trevor. I particularly like him. Very honest and direct."

Arlene tried for a little sarcastic laugh, but it came out a snort, a pig sound, and she could feel her face turn red because of it. "Yeah, he's all of that, all right. Only, you say it like it's a good thing."

"It is, I think. Now, what's this about paying

35

forward? I'm supposed to know something about that?"

Actually, she'd been hoping for a laugh, a smile, something besides his businesslike manner; a bad sense was forming of Mr. St. Clair looking down his nose at her in some way she could never entirely prove. "It has something to do with an assignment you gave out. That's what Trevor said. He said it was a project for your social studies class."

"Ah, yes. The assignment." He moved to the blackboard, and she swung out of his way, as though there were a big wind around him that kept her from getting too close. "I'll write it out for you, exactly as I did for the class. It's very simple." And he did.

THINK OF AN IDEA FOR WORLD CHANGE AND PUT IT INTO ACTION

He set his chalk down and turned back. "That's all it is. This 'paying forward' must be Trevor's own idea."

"That's all it is? That's all?" Arlene could feel a pressure building around her ears, that clean, satisfying anger she'd come here to vent. "You just want them to change the world. That's all. Well, I'm glad you didn't give them anything hard."

"Ms. McKinney—"

"Now, you listen here. Trevor is twelve years old. And you want him to change the world. I never heard such bull."

"First of all, it's a voluntary assignment. For extra credit. If a student finds the idea overwhelming, he or she need not participate. Second of all, what I want is for the students to reexamine their role in the world and think of ways one person can make a difference. It's a very healthy exercise."

"So is climbing Mount Everest, but that might be too much for the poor little guy too. Did you know Trevor has taken a homeless man under his wing and brought him into my house? A homeless man. A total stranger. This guy could have problems we know nothing about. What do you suggest I do about the trouble you've caused?"

"I suggest that you talk to Trevor. Lay down the house rules. Tell him when his efforts on this project conflict with safety. You do talk to him, don't you?"

"What kind of question is that? Of course I talk to him."

"It just seems odd that you would come all the way down here to find out what 'paying forward' is. When Trevor could tell you."

Leaving the room was becoming a more and more appealing option. "I guess this was a mistake." Obviously, nothing was being accomplished here.

"Ms. McKinney?" His voice hit her back a few steps into a long stride to safety and freedom.

She almost kept walking, but like ignoring a ringing phone, it was too contrary to human nature. She spun around to face this man, whom she now openly disliked.

"What?"

"I hope you'll forgive my asking this. But is Trevor's father dead?"

Arlene blinked as though she had been slapped. "No. Of course not." *I hope not.* "Did Trevor tell you that?"

"No. He said something strange. He said, 'We don't know where he is.' I thought maybe he was being euphemistic."

"Well, we *don't* know where he is."

"Oh. Well, I'm sorry. I just wondered."

Bewildered now, she struck for the door, and nothing could have stopped her. What a way to feel like a complete idiot.

Not only did she just admit that the father of her child hadn't so much as sent a Christmas card home, but now she'd have to go find a dictionary and look up the word "euphemistic." See what he'd just accused her son of being.

It better not have been an insult—that's all she could think.

From *The Diary of Trevor*

Sometimes I think this idea is gonna be so great. And maybe it is. But then other times I remember other things I thought would be great. Like when I was real young. Like ten or something. And now that I'm big, I can see what a crock it is. So then I think, *What if this all bombs out?* Then Mr. St. Clair won't be all impressed with me. And then in a few years I'll look back and think, *Boy, was I stupid.*

It's really hard to know what's a good idea when you're growing and these ideas don't hold still and neither do you.

Mom doesn't like Jerry. At all. Which is funny, because he's a lot like Dad. Except Dad is cleaner. But if Mom would let Jerry in the house, he'd be cleaner too. Maybe if she didn't keep letting Dad in, he'd look just like Jerry. Maybe, wherever he is, he already does.

CHAPTER FIVE

Jerry

He was just getting set to bunk down for the night, and there she was. Checking up on him.

He'd just gotten done on the truck. Taking the engine loose. Not from its mounts, but unhooking all the smog and the wiring. All of which there was way too much of. Not like the old days.

And he'd gone into the garage. Rolled out an old Oriental rug in a corner. Against a wall. Barely got his eyes closed.

She came in, flipped on the lights. Made him blink.

"It's only me, ma'am. Jerry. Just takin' a quick break. Just a nap. Then I'll get some more work done on your truck."

"I know you been living here, in my garage."

"No, ma'am. Just a quick nap."

"Then where are you staying?"

41

"Down at the shop where I work. They let me sleep on the couch in the waiting room."

"Get up. I'll drive you down there."

Darn.

They drove in silence down the Camino, the main street of town. A ghost town at this hour. The street was long and deserted, with traffic lights changing color for no reason he could see.

"Darn good car you got here." Old green Dodge Dart. *Serve you forever if you took care of it. Heck, even if you didn't.*

"That supposed to be some kind of sarcastic?"

"No, ma'am. I mean it for a fact. That slant six engine, best they ever made. Couldn't kill it if you tried." Silence. "I know you don't like me."

"It's not that."

"What, then?"

"Look, Jerry." Standing at a red light, idling. Even though there was no one around. No one to go on the green while they waited. "I'm trying to raise that boy on my own. No help from nobody. I can't watch him all the time."

"I don't mean no harm to your son."

"You don't *mean* none." Light turned, squeal of her tires. Just hit the gas too sudden.

42

She pulled up in front of the Quicky Lube & Tune.

It was cold out there. He didn't want to get out. Kind of thought he wouldn't have to. Anymore. No more sleeping out in the cold. He didn't really have a key to the shop. Would never in a million years have told his bosses he needed that couch to sleep on.

"Thanks for the ride, ma'am."

"I don't have anything against you personally. I don't."

"Right. Whatever."

He stepped out of the warm car. Into the wind. A minute later she was behind him.

"Look, Jerry. In a different world, who knows? We could have been friends even. It's just that—"

He spun around. She had to look at his face. Only for a second, then at his shoes. If only she wouldn't have looked at his shoes. He hadn't had enough money to replace the old sneakers. Saw a great pair of lace-up work boots but couldn't afford them. But tomorrow. Tomorrow would be payday.

"Pleased to hear you say that, ma'am. The way you been acting, I'da thought only one of us is people."

"I never meant that."

"Never *meant* it."

She turned to go back to the car. He turned to watch her go. So they both saw it. Like a long streak, starting at the top of the sky. Drifting down, but fast. Lighting up the night like lightning. A ball of fire with a tail.

"Holy cow," she said. "Did you see that? What was that, a comet?"

"Meteor maybe, I don't know. When I was a kid, we used to call that a falling star. I used to think if you saw one, you'd get your wish. You know, like all your dreams'd come true?"

She turned back to look at him. All softness in her face. Maybe it had never occurred to her that homeless people used to be kids. Or wanted their dreams to come true, like everybody.

She said, "Don't you hate moments like this?"

"What moments is those, ma'am?"

"When you get that feeling like we're all just the same?"

"No, ma'am. I like 'em."

"Well, good luck."

"Ma'am?"

"What?"

"I get my first paycheck tomorrow. And I'll go get a cheap room. Be out of your hair. Your boy won't be sorry he made the effort. I don't think you will either. I'll do just what I'm supposed to do. Pass it along, you know."

She stood there a long time, like she was trying to decide whether to say something or not. And she said it. "Will you explain to me about that? How that paying forward thing goes?"

He kind of blinked. "Didn't he tell you?"

"I didn't exactly ask."

From *Those Who Knew Trevor Speak*

So I explained "paying forward" to her. I got me a stick. Sketched it out in the dirt. In the dark. We both had to squint to see. It was cold, but she had a choice. Could have been home in a warm house. That made a difference. How do I know why?

I drew them three circles. And explained them. Like the kid explained them to me. "See, this one, that's me," I said. "These other two, I don't know. Two other somebodies, I guess. That he's gonna help. See, the trick is, it's something big. A big help. Like you wouldn't do for just anybody. Maybe your mother or your sister. But nobody else. He does that for me. I got to do it for three others. Other two, they got to do for three others. Those nine others,

45

they got to do it for three others. Each. That makes twenty-seven."

Now, I ain't so good with math. But that kid, he worked it out. It gets real big real fast. Like you can't believe how fast. Up in the thousands in no time.

So I'm on my knees there. Drawing all these circles in the dirt. Counting by threes. Running out of dirt. You can't believe how fast.

We're looking at these circles, thinking this whole thing could be great. Except it won't be. Because, well, we all know it won't. Because people, they won't really pay it forward. They will take your help, but that's all.

I know we were both thinking that.

And then the sky lit up again. So two big comets. That's a lot. Spooky.

You know, it's a big world out there. Bigger than we think.

Then she starts to tell me it's hard for her to talk to that kid. I couldn't believe it. Telling me. Me. She says he's just like his father that way. She hates to question him. Can't get mad at him. Don't want to seem like she don't trust him. So things just go by. She just lets 'em go by. She told me all this. It's like we were . . . I don't know . . . communicating. For the first time. About all kinds of stuff. It was so amazing. I told her I was gonna do big things. Maybe not big to somebody else. But from where I was. Get me an apartment. Drive a Dodge Dart. She said I could have hers. Dirt cheap. I told her again how tomorrow was payday. Payday. The day everything changes.

After a while it was all the same stuff we was saying. Over and over. But I liked it anyway. After a while she went home. But after that, the night was, like ... different. Like ... not so ... you know ... cold. Or something.

CHAPTER SIX

Reuben

When he arrived in his classroom on a Monday morning, Trevor was already seated. He'd taken a place in the front row like usual. They looked at each other briefly, Reuben sensing something unsaid on the boy's part.

"What's on your mind this morning, Trevor?"

"Mr. St. Clair? Are you married?"

"No. I'm not."

"Do you ever wish you were?"

Reuben remembered Trevor's mother standing in his classroom, remembered something she'd said when he'd called her son very honest and direct: "Yeah, he's all of that, all right. Only, you say it like it's a good thing." In fact, Reuben remembered Trevor's mother often. At odd moments, with no seeming connection, she would return in memory.

How, like a little storm cloud, she'd blown into his classroom one morning.

"That's a hard question to answer, Trevor. I mean, there's marriage and then there's marriage."

"Huh?"

"There are good ones and bad ones."

"Do you sometimes wish you had a good one?"

"Okay, I give up. What's this all about?"

"Nothing. I just wondered."

Mary Anne Telmin wandered in. Not surprising that she would be the next to arrive. She was the only other student Reuben knew for sure had accepted his extra-credit assignment, because she'd stayed after class one day and described it at great length. A recycling project. She was a cute, popular girl, the potential cheerleader type, about which Reuben tried to hold an open mind. But her approach to his class and assignment seemed insincere and staged, reminding him that Trevor's project remained secret.

And a good secret it might prove to be. Paying forward. He should have asked about that before the rest of the class began to arrive, but Trevor's strange questions had thrown him off his game.

• • •

After class Trevor filed out last, and Reuben raised a hand to flag him down, opened his mouth to call Trevor's name. But once again Trevor proved quicker on the draw.

"I want to talk to you again," Trevor said, turning and stopping in front of Reuben's desk. He jammed his hands deep into his pockets and waited until the last of the other students had gone. Little sweeps of his eyes and a slight rocking on his heels revealed something, but Reuben wasn't sure he could properly decode it. A little nervousness maybe.

Finally, convinced that they were alone, Trevor said, "My mom wants to know if you'll come to dinner tomorrow night."

"She said that?"

"Yeah. She said that."

And that little place in Reuben, the one he could never properly train, jumped up to meet her kindness, despite his caution. Maybe she didn't dislike him as much as he thought. But even Reuben's heart could sense when something didn't fit.

"Why does she want me to come to dinner?"

"I dunno. Why not?"

"She doesn't like me very much."

"You met my mom?"

"I met her temper, yes."

"Well . . . maybe she wants to talk about Jerry. My friend Jerry. He's part of my project. But she doesn't like him. At all. I think she wants you to help her, you know, sort of work it out. About that."

This invitation was becoming grounded now, in Reuben's mind, in something that made sense and fit with everything else he knew so far. "Couldn't we have a little private parent-teacher conference here at school?"

"Oh. Here at school. Well. I asked her. But she said, you know. She works so hard and all. Two jobs. She just said it would be nice if you could come over."

"I guess that would be okay. What time?"

"Uh. I'll have to ask her. I'll let you know tomorrow."

The following morning, early, just before his first class, it happened again. Lightning striking twice in the same place.

She was angry again, and Reuben wondered if she had ever settled down in between. He didn't even have to open his mouth this time, because her anger was all complete, needing only to be delivered. Reuben admired that in her. Envied it, actually, maybe even felt tempted to ask for lessons.

"Why did you tell my boy we had to meet at my house?"

"I didn't. I didn't say we had to meet at all."

"You didn't?" She stopped in mid-charge, obviously thrown, all fired up with no target. "Trevor told me to make chicken fajitas because you were coming for dinner. Because you wanted to talk to me about his project."

"Really?" *Interesting.* "He told me that *you* invited *me* over for dinner, and he thought it was because *you* wanted to talk to *me* about his project."

"Well, what the heck's he doing, then?" she said, as if to herself. As if Reuben were not in the room at all.

"Maybe he wants to talk to both of us about the project."

"But why not here at school?"

"He said you work two jobs and it would be easier if I came to the house."

"I'm here, aren't I?"

"I'm only telling you what he said."

"Oh. Okay. Why's he trying to get you over, then?"

It would be a risk to say it, but Reuben guessed that he probably would anyway. It would get her going again, most likely, which was okay, because he didn't mind her anger. It was clean and open and you could always see it coming.

"Yesterday morning he asked me if I was married. And then he asked me if I'd like to be."

"So?"

"I just thought . . ."

"What?"

"I just thought he might be trying to fix us up."

"Us?"

She seemed to freeze in place, everything running across her face at once, waiting to be read. Another risk, another defacing for which he'd left himself open. *Us? You must be joking.*

"I realize we're the world's most unlikely couple, but after all, he is just a boy."

He watched her stumble back up through herself, clumsily, to a place that could speak again. "Trevor would never do such a thing. He knows his daddy is gonna come home."

"Just guessing."

"Why did you even say you would come to dinner?"

"I felt guilty after you left last time. You were asking me to help straighten out some problems that might have been caused by my assignment. I'm afraid I was a little dismissive."

A beam of morning sun slanting through the window caught Arlene and made her brighter than anything else in the room.

"I know you don't like me." It was the last thing Reuben expected her to say, especially as he admired her. He felt transparent at almost all times, yet his intentions never seemed to be correctly read by those around him.

"What makes you think that?"

She made that noise again, that rude little snort. "You just said we're the most unlikely couple in the world. What does that mean, if you're not looking down on me?"

It means I assumed you were looking down on me. It means I knew you were thinking it, so I had to say it. But Reuben couldn't bring himself to give those answers, so she went on.

"You think I'm too stupid to see the way you look down on me? Well, I may not have your education and I may not talk good like you, but that don't mean I'm stupid."

"I never said you were stupid."

"You didn't have to."

"I never thought it, either. It never occurred to me to wonder how much education you have. I think you're being overly sensitive."

"What the heck would you know about what I'm feeling?"

"When it comes to oversensitivity, I'm something of an expert. Anyway, none of this was my idea, and if you don't want me in your house, I won't come."

"Uh, no. You know what? That's okay. Truth is . . ." Reuben knew from her pause, the strain in her face, that if she ever finished this sentence, she'd tell him something difficult. Something that was hard for her to say to anyone, but particularly to him. "Truth is, I'm not doing so good talking to him about this. I could use the help. Six o'clock?"

From *Those Who Knew Trevor Speak*

I went to her house. It wasn't at all what I expected. And that made me examine my own expectations and admit that perhaps in some small way I had been guilty of looking down on her. Though heaven knows I never meant to.

It was a modest house, but scrupulously clean inside and out, and fussed over, and tended. No plant life growing over the walkway. Not a single streak on those white-trimmed windowpanes. Except for a wrecked truck in the driveway, every part of her home brought back an expression my mother used to use in reference to herself: house proud.

I never expected her to remind me of my mother.

The whole thing made me nervous.

She answered the door looking distressingly nice. She was wearing this blousy, cottony dress in a flower print, as if she took dinner guests rather seriously. I stepped into her living room, holding flowers that I couldn't bring myself to give her. Frozen. Every part of me frozen. For the longest time neither of us could seem to talk about anything.

And then Trevor showed up, thank goodness.

As soon as Arlene cleared the dinner dishes from the table, Trevor ran to his room and got his calculator. He'd put off explaining his project all through dinner because, he said, it was too hard to explain without a calculator.

"This all started with something Daddy taught me."

Arlene's ears perked up at that, and she pulled her chair around, as if to watch the calculator over his shoulder.

"Remember that riddle he used to do? Remember that, Mom?"

"Well, I don't know, honey. He knew a lot of riddles."

Reuben's stomach felt warm and nicely full. He watched them both across the table, feeling surprisingly relaxed. The flowers he'd brought her sat in a vase on the table. Not roses—that would have been too personal, too much. A mix of dried flowers and sunny things, daisies and the like, which he'd presented with an apology for having made a bad first impression. Intended only as a friendly gesture, it had embarrassed her and made them both feel awkward. It had been a mistake, one he'd take back if he could, and every glance at them sitting in the porcelain vase reminded him that he could not.

"Remember that one about working for thirty days?"

"No, Trevor, I don't think I do."

"Remember, he said if you were going to work for somebody for thirty days, and you had a choice—you could take a hundred dollars a day, or you could take a dollar the first day, and then it would be doubled every day. I said I'd take a hundred dollars a day. But he said I'd lose out. So I worked it out on my calculator. A hundred dollars a day for thirty days is three thousand dollars. But if you double that dollar every day, you'd make over five hundred million on your last day. Not to mention everything between. That's how I thought of my idea for Mr. St. Clair's class. You see, I do something real good for three people. And then when they ask how they can pay it back, I say they have to pay it forward. To three more people. Each. So nine people get helped. Then those people have to do twenty-seven." He turned on the calculator, punched in a few numbers. "Then it sort of spreads out, see. To eighty-one. Then two hundred forty-three. Then seven hundred twenty-nine. Then two thousand one hundred eighty-seven. See how big it gets?"

"But, honey. There's just one little problem with that."

"What, Mom?"

"I'm sure Mr. St. Clair will explain it to you."

Reuben jumped at the mention of his name. "I will?"

"Yes. Tell him what's wrong with the plan."

"I think your mother is upset because . . . well, it's about the homeless man. She's . . . worried. About that situation."

"No, no. Not that. Trevor, I know I gave you a hard time about Jerry, but then I had a long talk with him. And I might've been wrong about him.

58

He's a pretty nice guy. Besides, I think he got a place to live. He hasn't been around for a few days."

Trevor's forehead furrowed down and he clicked off the calculator. "I went by his work. They said he never came back after they paid him."

"Honey, I'm sorry. See, that is the very part Mr. St. Clair is about to explain."

Reuben took his napkin off his lap and threw it on the table. This pattern between Arlene and her son—it had come deadly clear. *"Here's Mr. St. Clair, son, to tell you all the things you don't want to hear." I'm sorry, Ms. McKinney. If you want your son to believe that people are basically selfish and irresponsible, you'll have to tell him so yourself.* He smiled tightly and shook his head, saying nothing.

She fixed him with a look that burned in silence.

"Well, Trevor," she said. "I think it's a good project. Tell us more about it."

So Trevor explained, with the help of his calculator, how big this thing could become. Somewhere around the sixteenth level, at which he'd involved 43,046,721 people, the calculator proved smaller than Trevor's optimism. But he was convinced that in just a few more levels, the numbers would be larger than the population of the world. "Then you know what happens? Then everybody gets helped more than once. And it gets bigger even faster."

"What do you think, Mr. St. Clair?" Arlene clearly wanted something from him, but he wasn't sure from minute to minute what that something might be.

"I think it's a noble idea, Trevor. A big effort. Big efforts lead to good grades. How do you feel about the fact that Jerry is gone?"

Trevor sighed. From the look on Arlene's face, Reuben had done his job correctly for a change.

"It's okay, I guess. Except I just have to start all over, is all. It's okay, though. I already got other ideas."

"Like what, honey?" Arlene asked in that sugary voice she slipped into when questioning her own son.

"It's a secret. Can I be excused?"

Arlene caught Reuben's eye again, begging for something. As if she could not just say, *No, young man, we are not done here.* Reuben only shrugged.

"Okay, run along, then, honey."

Trevor charged in the direction of his bedroom, but as he barreled by Reuben's seat, Reuben took him gently by the sleeve and pulled him over close enough that Arlene, on the other side of the table, hopefully would not hear.

"You can't orchestrate love, Trevor."

"What's 'orchestrate'?"

"You can't make it happen for somebody else."

"Doesn't that have something to do with music?"

"Not always."

"Oh. You can't, huh? I mean. Oh. Okay. That wasn't my idea, though. Anyway."

"Just checking."

Reuben loosed his sleeve and Trevor disappeared.

Reuben looked up to see Arlene glaring across the table with that mixture of stress and anger and rocket fuel to which he was becoming nicely accustomed.

"What'd you say to him?"

"It's a secret. May I be excused?"

From *The Diary of Trevor*

Mom and Mr. St. Clair like each other. I just know it. What I can't figure out is, why don't they know it? It's right there, and I just feel like shaking them and saying, *Oh, just admit it.* Mr. St. Clair would be nice to her, I think. I think he'd give his entire heart to somebody who would say, *You know, that's a nice half a face you got there.* You know, like the glass is half full instead of . . . well, you know. He's sad about his face. I think if he wasn't, he could admit it better when he liked somebody. But then my mom has a great face, and she's doing it too. Go figure.

What if the world really changed because of my project? Wouldn't that be the coolest thing? Then everybody would say, *Who cares about his face? He's the best teacher in the world, that's what matters.* That would be so cool.

I think the best shot I got now for my project is Mrs. Greenberg. Jerry's gone, and Mr. St. Clair says you can't orchestrate love, which made it sound like I was trying to wave a baton around or something. But so far it looks like he's right.

But a garden. A garden holds still for all that orchestra stuff.

CHAPTER SEVEN

Mrs. Greenberg

Her late husband, Martin, had believed in miracles, but the cancer took him just the same. Since he'd gone, she'd tried to bring that belief around again, thinking it to be natural to the family, divinely intended to live in her little blue-gray house.

And this evening, for the first time in years, it sat on the porch swing with her as she sipped her iced tea. It smiled for her and through her, and she smiled back.

A miracle in the shape of her garden.

Lately, she'd begun to dream of waking up, stretching and flexing through the pain in her arthritic joints, easing to the window to discover that, as if by magic, the garden was once again whole. And now, in the dusk of a cool spring evening, the garden was whole. Trimmed, the grass mowed, beds laid with fresh cedar chips, freshly raked, bags of leaves and trimmings bundled at the curb.

Not an unexplained miracle, exactly, because she'd watched the neighbor boy do it all, day after day. Barely a head taller than he, she'd stood at his side and shown him the junctions at which rose-bushes begged to be trimmed and aphids to be sprayed, and the weeds that had to come out, and the ground cover meant to be cut back, watered, encouraged to flourish.

But miracles can and do have middlemen, she decided, and then she noticed that her iced tea tasted sweeter than usual that night, though made to the same proportions, and that the cold glass did not ache her arthritis the way it usually did. And as if to dampen this perfect balance just the moment she'd discovered it, her son, Richard, came up the walk for his bimonthly visit.

He'd been a smart boy, Richard, a brilliant boy, but seemingly with no payoff, unlike the neighbor boy, who appeared quite simple and average in intelligence, yet seemed to prove otherwise with his very willingness to be where he was needed.

At forty-two Richard was not a willing man, nor was he serious, unless anxious counts, and not particularly cheerful or helpful. But maybe intelligence is not associated with cheerful willingness; too bad she could not trade in Richard's intelligence at this late date. Seemed its only real purpose was to lose him every job he ever tried, being too good as he was for all of them. And she had no more money to lend him, and would not if she could.

He stood on her porch step. "Hi, Mom."

"So? What do you think?"

"About what?"

"The garden."

He spun on the heels of his two-tone leather boots and flipped his dark glasses up to the top of his thin hairline.

"Shoot. You paid somebody. I told you I'd do it."

"I didn't pay. The neighbor boy did it for free."

"Very funny."

"He did."

"It must've taken hours."

"He's been working for days. You haven't been around."

"I told you I'd do it."

"Yes. You told me. But you didn't do it."

At first Trevor had just come by to talk, and that was good enough, and Mrs. Greenberg had never expected more.

She was right near the end of his paper route, which he changed around just a little so her house would be the very last. He'd leave his big, heavy old bicycle on its side on her lawn and bring the paper right to her door and knock, knowing as he did that it was a bother for her to go out after it. She was so pleased by his thoughtful attention that she always offered him a glass of cherry Kool-Aid, which she bought specially for him, and he'd sit at her kitchen table and talk to her. About school mostly, and football, and then a special project he had thought up for his social studies class, and how he needed more people he could help, and she said she had some gardening to be done, though she couldn't afford to pay much.

He said she wasn't to pay anything at all to him, and what she paid to others needn't be money, unless that was what she had plenty of. And then he drew some circles for her on a piece of paper, with her name in one, and told her about paying forward.

"It's like random acts of kindness," she'd said, but he disagreed. It was not random, not at all, and therein lay its beauty, built right into the sweet organization of the deal.

It was a foggy Saturday morning when he came

by, six o'clock sharp as promised, and they'd stood in the mist in the front yard, the blue-gray paint peeling from her worried little house, and the smell of damp in the air, and little drips from the oak trees overhead cool in her hair.

He'd touched the roses as if they were puppies with their eyes still closed, or rare old books edged in gold leaf, and she knew he'd love her garden and it would love him back. And that something was being returned to her which had been away too long and had kept too much of her away with it.

"How is the project going so far?" she'd said, because she could see it was important to him, a subject he liked to talk a lot about.

His brow furrowed and he said, "Not so good, Mrs. Greenberg. Not so good." He said, "Do you think that maybe people won't really pay it forward? That maybe they'll just say they will, or even sort of mean to, but maybe something'll go wrong, or maybe they'll just never get around to it?"

She knew it was a genuine problem in his mind. So she said, "I can only in truth speak for myself, Trevor, and say that I really will get around to it and take it every bit as seriously as I know you do."

She could still remember his smile.

He'd worked so hard that day and wouldn't

even stop for a Kool-Aid break but once, and when he'd finished, she tried to slip a five-dollar bill in his hand, above and beyond and in no way connected to paying it forward, but he wouldn't hear of it.

He worked all weekend, and four after-school and after-paper-route days, on the garden, and said next week he would come around and paint her fence and window boxes and porch railing with two fresh coats of white.

She wondered if her son, Richard, would notice the difference.

She walked to the grocery store slowly, loosening her tight joints and muscles as they warmed to the strain.

It was late dusk on the Camino, with the car headlights glowing spooky in the half-light as she pulled her little two-wheeled wire cart behind her over the sidewalk cracks. Mrs. Greenberg always took the same route to the same store, being comforted by sameness.

Terri was working as a checker that evening and Matt as a bagger, two of her favorite people in the world. No more than twenty, either one of them, but quick with a smile for an older woman, no looking down on her, always thinking to ask about her day, her arthritis, and still listening when she gave the answer.

She bought twelve cans of cat food and a five-pound bag of dry cat chow, for the strays who counted on her, and cherry Kool-Aid for the boy, and Richard's favorite brand of soda, and tea and skinless chicken breasts and bran cereal for herself.

All the while thinking, *Terri and Matt, that's two who probably could be counted on to pass it along, and maybe that nice lady at the North County Cat Shelter would make a fitting third.* Richard would have a cow, but maybe tough love was just what he needed, and with that thought fresh in her mind, she returned to the cooler and put his soda back on the shelf. He could drink Kool-Aid or iced tea, or go home and take his money problems with him.

"Good evening, Mrs. Greenberg," Terri said, running the groceries across the scanner. "I drove by your house today. The garden looks wonderful."

It pleased her in an uplifting way, like a dance with a good-looking boy in high school, that someone besides herself should notice and care.

"Isn't it wonderful?" she said. "Trevor McKinney did all that. Such a good boy. Do you know him?"

Terri didn't imagine that she did, but it obviously pleased her to see Mrs. Greenberg so beaming, and

Matt too, who mirrored back her own smile as he bagged her cat food.

"Nice to see you so happy tonight, Mrs. Greenberg." He loaded her little cart carefully so it would balance just right.

It would be nice to see Matt happy too, though by design she would not be around to see it. Young people needed a little nest egg, for college maybe, though it would not be enough for tuition, maybe books and clothes or whatever they might choose to spend it for, because she felt they could both be trusted.

And that nice lady at the cat shelter, she would put it right back into spaying and neutering and other vet costs. No doubting her priorities.

Yes, she thought, back out in the crisp, clean-smelling night. *It's right.* She'd make the calls first thing in the morning.

Her chest first began to hurt on the way home. Not her heart, but more her lungs, like a bad congestion, and she stopped often to catch her breath. She was not such an old woman, she had to remind herself, just over retirement age, but since losing Martin, her body seemed to turn in on itself, as though it couldn't wait. The arthritis had tripled its hold since then, and she'd catch any little thing that was going around.

Stopping often to rest, she took a detour, which she never did, by Trevor McKinney's house. Such a nice little house, with a curvy shingle roof, heavy with vegetation but never overgrown-looking. Too bad about that twisted, awful truck in the driveway. Mrs. Greenberg imagined Trevor's mother must want it gone, want the simple beauty of her place back, maybe even dreamed of it the way she herself had dreamed for her garden.

They had company, she saw, stopping for breath at the walkway. A white Volkswagen Beetle, nicely cared for, parked out front. A new gentleman friend. Good. She'd seen the old one, didn't think much of the type.

And she could see, through the window, into the brightly lit dining room, the right side of his face in profile. A well-dressed black man, so handsome and refined.

Well, good, then. Good for them.

Mrs. Greenberg hoped Trevor's mother wouldn't listen to anybody, wouldn't let any small minds get in her way. They had tried to tell her not to marry Martin, because he was a Jewish boy, but she wouldn't listen, and he'd been the best husband a woman could ask for. A good man is a good man.

Maybe Trevor's mother would get married. Nice for the boy if she did. She'd never met Trevor's mother but knew she would like her, because look who she had raised. A boy who could love a garden for a sick, arthritic woman who couldn't love it enough.

"You have a good woman there," she said quietly, out loud, to the handsome, refined man in the window, who of course did not hear. "A good woman with a good boy. You take care of them. I know you will."

She arrived home at last, winded and sore chested.

She took a hot bath and laid herself, coughing, to bed, knowing that whatever happened now, the garden was tended. The porch would take a coat of paint. Tomorrow she'd make some calls, some arrangements. After that, it didn't matter.

Everything was tended, or would be by then.

CHAPTER EIGHT

Arlene

She slipped in to say good night to Trevor the minute Mr. St. Clair left. And he didn't leave a moment too soon. What was it, anyway, about that man that always made her feel she was missing the boat on something, and why couldn't she shake the notion that he was doing it on purpose?

Trevor lay on his bed, doing homework in his lap. "Gotta go to work, honey. You still got the number by the phone?"

"Sure, Mom."

"And Loretta's?"

"Know it by heart. You know I'm not scared. I never am."

"I know, honey. But I am."

"I'm a big kid, Mom."

"You sure are, honey. That you are."

She sat on the edge of his bed combing curly

73

strands of hair off his forehead with her fingers. She knew he probably didn't like it, smacking as it did of the preening one gives a much younger child, but he did not complain.

"Honey?"

"Yeah, Mom?"

"You weren't trying to . . ."

"What?"

"No. Never mind. I gotta go."

"No, really. What?"

"You weren't trying to . . . fix me up with Mr. St. Clair. Were you? I was pretty sure you weren't."

"Why? Don't you like him?"

It hit her in the stomach like a fastball, something she could really feel, to know that he had. Even though she wasn't sure why it should seem so important. And then, looking down at Trevor's homework, she saw the sheet of paper with Trevor's idea sketched out on it. Circles like the ones Jerry had drawn in the dirt, between comets, when they both believed for a flash of a moment that his life could really change.

The circles were blank, all except the top three. One had Jerry's name written inside, then scratched out, which made Arlene suddenly, overwhelmingly sad, as if his chance had gone up just that quickly. The second said Mr. St. Clair, also scratched out, which also made her feel something, though she couldn't name it. The third said Mrs. Greenberg, which, thankfully, meant nothing at all.

Her own words didn't sound quite right at first. "Well, actually, Trevor, no. I don't think I do like him. He makes me kind of nervous. Why? Do you like him?"

"Yeah. Sure I do."

"Why?"

"I don't know. I think it's because you can say things to him. And then he says things back. Just real simple like that. Whatever you think of, you can just say. That's good, right?"

"Well, I guess so, but . . . honey, I just don't get why you would do that."

"I think he's lonely, Mom. And I know you are. And you always said you don't judge people by how they look."

"No. That's right. You don't." She learned so much from these little talks with her son. He always swore he'd learned it from her and was only mirroring it back, but somehow the wisdom of her own advice surprised her as it came out of his mouth

75

and left her wondering if she was wise enough to heed it. It happened this way every time. "And it's not that at all, honey, it's not about looks in any way, it's just that, well, you know as well as anybody that your daddy'll be back one of these days."

He didn't answer at first, just looked up at her with an expression that made it hard for her to breathe. If pressed to put words to it, she'd be tempted to call it a look of pity, but surely he hadn't meant it to be as harsh as all that. "Mom." She so didn't want to hear the next thing he'd say but felt too tongue-tied to stave it off. "Mom. It's been more'n a year."

"So?"

"Mom. He's not coming back."

And she'd been so careful to never let those words into her home, her mind. But now here they were, having to be fought with desperate means.

So Arlene did something she'd never done, not in twelve years; she raised the back of her hand to her own son and slapped him across the mouth. She tried to stop the hand before it quite hit home, but the signal didn't go through in time.

He looked at her without anger, without adding one tiny stick of kindling to the shame that already threatened to burn her at the stake.

She'd never hit Trevor, promised herself she never would.

And then, to make matters worse, so unequipped was she to deal with her own shame that she spun on her heels and left him alone.

Her eyes kept darting to the clock, hoping for a moment free to call Trevor before he fell asleep, but that moment wouldn't seem to come.

When she finally got a break, she used the phone in the kitchen.

Trevor picked up on the fourth ring, right before her heart attack set in. "Honey. You okay?"

"Sure, Mom. I'm always okay."

"Were you asleep?"

"Not yet. I'll go in a minute, though. I was reading that World War Two book."

"Trevor, I am so, so sorry. I am so ashamed that I hit you, I just cannot say." She paused, hoping for something, anything, that would relieve her of the duty to continue. "If there's ever anything I can do to make it up. Anything at all."

"Well."

"Anything."

"I don't think you'd go for it."

"Anything."

"Will you take me to visit Jerry?"

"Do you even know where he is, honey?"

"Um . . . yeah. But you won't like it."

The woman in the front cubicle of the county jail wore her red nails so long, she had to type with the eraser end of a pencil. She sat with her legs crossed, chewing gum with clicking sounds Arlene found irritating.

Arlene tightened her grip on Trevor's shoulder.

"Name?"

"Arlene McKinney."

"And you're here to visit . . ."

"Jerry Busconi."

"Can I see some ID, please?"

Arlene slid her driver's license across the counter.

"Wait in there, please," the woman said, sliding the license back and gesturing with one amazing nail.

Arlene stood with Trevor in a corner, clutching at his sleeve, and wondered if these people would think Jerry was her husband, and if so, why she minded so much that they would.

Ten minutes ticked by, each feeling like a day, then they were allowed into a room with a long table, a long line of chairs, Plexiglas dividers, and telephones. Just like in the movies.

A few more long minutes.

No new prisoners, no Jerry, just more waiting, more holding Trevor's arm, maybe tightly enough to hurt.

A guard shuffled by behind the divider. She leaned forward and tapped on the glass, and the uniformed man picked up the phone. "Problem?"

"What happened to Jerry Busconi?"

"He's not coming out."

"What do you mean, he's not coming out? My son and I came all the way down here to visit him."

"Can't make him take a visitor. Said he wasn't in the mood."

Wasn't in the mood. Jerry Busconi wasn't in the mood to see the boy who was always in the mood to give him all the proceeds of his own hard after-school work. *Mood, it takes. That's rich. Yeah, that's a good one.* "Can I leave a note?"

"Front desk."

"Thanks."

Jerry,

I cannot bring myself to say "dear" because right at the moment you are not dear to me

79

at all. I can forgive you for getting in trouble because we all mess up, and I am no exception. But this little boy who helped you and counted on you came down here to see how you were, and you were not in the mood. Which I think makes you eighteen different kinds of chicken.

It's always easy to get mad on his behalf—in fact, it's sort of a specialty of mine—but truth is, I'm mad at what you did to me, too. Telling me all your hopes and dreams so I couldn't not like you, because this would be a whole lot easier if I had never liked or trusted you, but you have taken even that small comfort away from me.

I don't trust many people, and then when I make an exception, seems it's always the wrong one.

Get your sorry self out of this place as soon as you can and then do what you said you would do for my boy and his school project, which is very important to him.

I believe people can change, even though it seems they never do, but if you can't face us today, that says a lot about what you will do later. I don't believe in shooting stars, and if I ever had, I would not believe in them no more, and that is what you have done to this family.

Think about that while you're doing your time.

My boy would like to write something on this note when I'm done, which I am.

Arlene McKinney

Hi Jerry,

Hope you are okay and the food is not too terrible. Do you get to watch TV? Will you write me a letter from the state pen? Nobody ever did before.

Well, gotta go. Mom's ticked.

Your friend,

Trevor

From *The Diary of Trevor*

I wonder where people go when they die. They have to go somewhere. Right?

I mean, it would be just too weird to think about Mrs. Greenberg not being anywhere. That would just be too sad.

So I've decided that she's still out there somewhere. Because I've decided I can think whatever I want about it. Because I've noticed that everybody thinks something different about it. So I figure that means you can think what you want.

Course, that means I'm gonna have to keep that garden real nice. And the cats! I just thought. Somebody's gonna have to keep feeding all those wild cats. I wonder how much cat food costs.

Anyway. You know what? Even this way, it's still sad.

CHAPTER NINE

Reuben

He'd been in this house for three months, but nothing was unpacked. Almost nothing. The big bed was set up, made, and comfortable, so he spent a lot of time on it, grading papers, eating off his lap, and watching the news.

He made his way through the sea of boxes to the kitchen, took a small carton of ice cream out of the freezer, and proceeded to eat standing up, right out of the carton, with a plastic spoon, the cat weaving around and through his legs. It made him feel lonely, but then, so did unpacking.

The phone rang and proved difficult to find. It was Trevor.

"Is it okay that I called you at home? I got the number from information."

"Is something wrong, Trevor? Are you in some kind of trouble? Is your mother there?"

"It's nothing like that. I'm okay. It's just my proj-ect. It's not going so good. At all. It just got a lot worse. Something bad happened. Can I talk to you about it?"

"Of course you can, Trevor."

"Good. Where do you live?"

Reuben let the receiver slip down and looked around. "Maybe I could meet you somewhere, Trevor, like the park. Or the library."

"It's okay. I'll ride my bike over. Where do you live?"

So Reuben gave him the address, on Rosita, just off San Anselmo, thinking they could talk on the front porch.

To be extra safe, he called Trevor's mother, who was listed in the phone book, to explain where Trevor would be and why. She wasn't home, and Reuben had no idea if she worked on Saturdays, but he left a message on her answering machine. Just in case.

Trevor dumped his bike on its side on Reuben's lawn. Reuben realized he had never seen Trevor upset, so far as he knew.

He stood on the bottom porch step in khaki shorts and a 49ers T-shirt. "Mrs. Greenberg died."

"I'm so sorry, Trevor," he said, offering the boy a straight-backed chair on the porch. "Come sit down and tell me about her. Who she was to you."

"She was for my project. She was, like, my last chance." Then he stopped himself, as if ashamed, and took the chair offered him. "That didn't sound right. I didn't mean I was upset about my project, when she died and all. It's not that. It's both. I mean, she really was going to pay it forward. She told me. And then she died. I went over to her house this morning. I always take the paper right up to her door. But the last couple days it's like she's not home. But she's always home. So today it was Saturday, so I just waited. And then the mailman came, and he said she hadn't taken the mail out of her box for three days. He said her monthly check was in there and it wasn't like her not to get it right away. So then we knocked on her neighbor's door, and they called her son, and he came over and opened the door. And she was in bed, just like she was sleeping. Only she wasn't sleeping. She was dead."

Trevor stopped for a breath.

"I'm sorry, Trevor. That must have been hard for you."

"The project is almost due. Jerry got arrested.

He wouldn't even come out when we went to visit. And my mom still thinks my daddy is gonna come back. The whole thing is a bust, Mr. St. Clair."

"I'm not sure I follow the part about your mother." He halfway did but hoped Trevor might elaborate.

"Oh. Well. It doesn't matter. But what am I gonna do for my project?"

Reuben shook his head. It hurt to watch a boy lose his idealism. Almost as much as it had hurt when he'd lost his own. "I guess you just report your effort. I'm grading on effort, not results."

"I wanted results."

"I know you did, Trevor."

He watched the boy pick at a seam on the cuff of his shorts.

"I didn't just want a good grade. I really wanted the world to get better."

"I know you did. It's a tough assignment. That's part of its lesson, I'm afraid. We all want to change the world, and sometimes we need to learn that it's harder than we think."

"I really do feel bad about Mrs. Greenberg, though. She was a nice lady. I don't think she was really old. I mean, sort of old. But not that old. We used to talk."

Reuben looked up to see an old green Dodge Dart pull up to the curb and Arlene McKinney step out.

He watched her march up the walkway, up the steps to his porch. All outward confidence covering awkward nerves. And it struck him then, for the first time, how much alike they really were.

"I know you don't like me," she'd said. *"I know you're looking down on me."* So there it was. He acted defensive toward her because he assumed she found him ugly. She acted defensive toward him because she assumed he found her stupid.

"Now, Trevor," she said, "I bet Mr. St. Clair's got better things to do than hear about your troubles on a nice Saturday morning. You can talk to me, you know."

"You weren't home." Trevor studied his scuffed high-tops.

"I didn't mind, Ms. McKinney. Really. I just wanted you to know where he was."

"Well, I thank you for that, but we'll just be going now." She motioned with a hand to her son, who followed her off the porch obediently.

"Arlene." He hadn't known he was about to call her back, had never intended to use her first name. She must have been surprised too. She spun around, looked at him for the longest time. Really looked at him, as though seeing something she hadn't seen before. And it made him uncomfortable to feel so transparent.

"Trevor, wait for me in the car," she said quietly, and rejoined Reuben on the porch.

Reuben was no longer sure he could express his revelation; still, he had no choice but to try.

"When you first met me, and you thought I was looking down my nose at you . . . I just want you to know something."

She waited patiently, face slightly turned up to him. She reflected a pleasant expectance. She didn't dislike him. She just wanted him to like her. It was right there on her face.

"I have a hard time meeting people. I'm very sensitive about— Well, I tend to think I repel people. I mean, I do. But I was being defensive. That's what I'm trying to say. I wasn't looking down on you. I was being defensive because I thought you were looking down on me."

"Really?" A skinless, unguarded question.

"Really."

"Well, thank you. That's nice." She moved to the porch rail, glanced at the car and her waiting son. "No, really, that's nice. I appreciate that you told me that. It's kind of funny, really. I mean, here we are being all cold to each other. You don't think I'm dumb? Really?"

"Not at all."

"I don't talk good like you. Talk well, I mean. I could, I guess. I know how to talk right. I just sorta got out of the habit. Maybe you could come over for dinner again some night."

"Maybe."

Maybe? Reuben felt surprised to hear himself say it. Maybe. Actually, he'd wanted to say no. Now that she had turned her eyes up to him, hopeful and childlike, flattered to win his approval, he could not get far enough away from her.

She stared at him for a moment, then marched purposefully back to her car and drove off without comment.

That should have been a safe, comfortable end to everything, but the following Thursday evening he ran into her at the market. Just dropped into a long-ish line with his ice cream and his TV dinners and found himself looking at the back of her head.

It seemed to Reuben as though one could look at the back of someone else's head quietly, without being noticed, but apparently, he did it wrong, because she immediately turned around.

"Oh, you," she said, and that was it. She turned back, and they both waited in excruciating silence, watching Terri and Matt scan and bag groceries.

She looked briefly over her shoulder at Reuben on her way out of the store.

Then she was gone, and he breathed deeply, a man just having found his way to safety from grave and immediate danger.

He found her in the parking lot, leaning on his car. "You know what your problem is?" she said.

It was the old Arlene, and it felt good to Reuben to have her back, that little lightning bolt of indignation all ready to read him the riot act about one thing or another.

"No. I don't. What is my problem?"

"Your problem is, you're so quick to think nobody wants you, you don't even give 'em a chance. I couldn't reject you if I tried. You're too fast for me."

"Thank you, Arlene. That was very informative."

He moved for his driver's door, and she peeled away, out of his path, as he knew she would. He set his groceries on the passenger seat, got in, and slammed the door. But she wasn't gone. She stood by his window as he fired up the little engine, and before he could drive away, she tapped on the glass.

He rolled the window halfway down.

"So," she said. "You want to go out, or what?"

"Yes and no."

"What kind of answer is that?"

"The honest kind. What do you want me to say?"

"I want you to say, 'I'm not busy on Sunday night, Arlene. Maybe you and me could take in a movie or something.'"

Reuben sighed. He put the Volkswagen in gear, popped it out again. "Arlene, would you like to go to a movie this Sunday?"

He didn't mean it to, but it came out sounding petulant, like a little boy who'd just been ordered to apologize when he wasn't feeling one bit sorry.

"Yes, I would. But I bet I'm gonna be sorry I ever started with this."

"I'll put a couple of dollars on that too," Reuben said, but he was half a block away before he said it.

CHAPTER TEN

Matt

The store closed at nine, and he wasted no time breaking for the door. Three times when he checked the clock, he'd been sure it was broken, but another minute had eventually ticked away. Not for any special reason did the time go so slowly. Not much more than usual. Work always crawled by.

He'd parked his motorcycle behind the shop, on the hill. It made so much noise, and the owner always gave him a dirty look if he idled it too close to the store. It didn't have an electric starter, or rather, the one it had didn't work. So he had to kick it over. And it didn't have a neutral light, so he had to rock it back and forth a bit to make sure it wasn't in gear. Which was hard on the hill. Hard to coast it, hard to be sure.

Thinking it was in neutral, he straddled the bike, jumped on the kick lever, and the bike, still in first gear, rolled forward off the side stand and fell with him.

Now there'd be another three weeks of gas-tank-shaped bruise on the inside of his thigh, but that wasn't the worst of it. Straining to pick the bike up again, Matt saw he'd broken the front brake lever. Hit the handlebar and sheared it right off. And the back brake wasn't any too good. He closed his eyes and thought about screaming. But it was a quiet night, the houses in this neighborhood filled with quiet people. Nobody liked trouble.

Besides, he'd tried that once. Stood in the street and yelled at the bike, called it every name he could think of. Hadn't fixed a thing.

He turned the bike around, straddled it again, coasted it down the hill. Popped the clutch and roll-started it. If only he'd thought of that to begin with.

He cruised the Camino at twenty-five, half pulled over to the curb. That way, if he had to stop suddenly, he'd have a fighting chance. Five guys in a lowrider Chevy slowed beside him, asked if he needed training wheels. It was a worse day than most, but not in a whole different ballpark.

Only thing Matt hated more than going to work was going home and listening to the fighting. He had a tent in the overgrown backyard for when things got really bad. At nineteen, he knew he needed a place of his own, but it was not that easy. Everybody wanted first and last month's rent, nobody wanted to pay more than $4.25 an hour for anybody who was anything-teen.

He pulled into his driveway, cut the engine. Put the bike up on the center stand. From out there, he could already hear it, but he went inside all the same.

Then he saw the letter on the dining room table. He never got mail. And it was from someone he'd never heard of. Ida Greenberg. Weird. A big, thick envelope. Pages and pages mailed to him from Ida Greenberg.

Whoever she was.

Dearest Matthew,

If you are reading this, I have passed away. I left this letter in with some personal things, with a note to my son, Richard, asking him to mail it after I'm gone.

This morning I made some phone calls. To my insurance company and to my lawyer. I had to make a very big decision, and I made it. I have a $25,000 life insurance policy, and I decided not to leave it to my son. I don't trust that he would use it the right way.

I have decided to split it three ways. $8,333 will go to you. The same amount to Terri, whom I also like very much, and the other third to that nice lady at the cat shelter, because she is selfless and does good work.

This leaves one dollar for Richard. He will kick and he will be very temperamental. I think you may have to attend the reading of the will, and it may not be pleasant. But I have worked it out carefully with my lawyer. Richard can contest it, and he probably will, but he won't win. We've sealed it all up carefully.

You may do what you want with this money, but I'm trusting you to use it well. Not selflessly, just well. Definitely spend it on yourself. But don't waste it.

If you want to know why I chose you, it's because you always had a nice smile, and you asked how I was feeling. And then you listened to the answer. You never made me feel like I didn't matter or like I wasn't there.

Now. The money is not exactly free. I have done you a big favor. Well, the biggest favor it's in my power to do. I know $8,333 doesn't go as far as it used to. But it's all I have. The house is mortgaged up to the hilt, and my

Social Security payments expire when I do.

Here's what I want you to do. Do a very big favor for three people. It doesn't have to be money. Just give them something that is as big to you as $8,333 is to me. And when they try to pay you back, tell them instead to pay it forward.

Give your time, if you have to, or your compassion. Lots of people have money but not that.

You are a nice boy. Enjoy the money.

Best wishes,

Ida Greenberg

Just a little over six weeks later he had it in his hand. He'd already put a fifty-dollar deposit on the apartment so the guy wouldn't rent it to somebody else. He spent the night there, in a sleeping bag. He had a decent bed at his folks' house but no way to move it yet.

It was quiet.

When he opened the window, he was right out on the slanting roof, because this apartment used to be an attic once, before somebody divided up the house. And he sat out on the roof in the dark, in the cold, just liking the quiet. He saw trees and nothing else. Just the side of a hill covered with trees. And a sliver of yellow moon gleaming through. Which was more than enough.

So he sat there for a while, wondering where people go when they die and what he could possibly do for somebody else that would mean as much as this $8,333 meant to him. And what to buy with the rest of the money. And whether Mrs. Greenberg would know. He didn't figure she would; it seemed corny to think she was watching. But he'd never known anyone who died, never thought much about it before, and he wasn't all that completely positive that she wouldn't know. Unlike the $8,333, it wasn't something he could take to the bank.

The next morning he drove his old piece of junk motorcycle to the Honda dealer in San Luis Obispo. They said they'd give him $75 in trade. The first thing that caught his eye was a real pretty, brand-new 750. With a windshield, and all space-age aerodynamic in red and white, with a custom paint job. He sat on it. He shouldn't have sat on it. It cost almost $7,000. Which was just so close to all he had left after first and last month's rent and that big security deposit. But, man. It was more than pretty. It was, like . . . power. But it was too much.

97

They also had a new 350, like his old one but seven model years newer and no miles. And a neutral light and an electric starter. And then, for $3,500, they had a 250, also with a nice custom paint job, also brand new. A 350 . . . a 250. The 250 would go fast enough to ride on the highway. Just barely. And if he could go faster, maybe that would just get him a ticket, which he could not afford. Insurance ate up too much of his paycheck as it was.

Then he sat on the 750 again, feeling that power. Nobody was going to pull up beside him while he was on this bad boy to talk about training wheels. But it was too much. It was most of the old lady's money. That was all she had, that insurance, like someone cashed in her life and that's what it all added up to.

This was giving him a headache.

He rode his old piece of junk to the Taco Bell. Had a breakfast burrito, thought some more.

Then he went back and bought the 250.

And on the way home stopped at Cuesta College to get a catalogue of all their classes. And sat on his brand-new little bike in the parking lot and leafed through the catalogue, and it was so cool because there was no possible combination of classes that he could not afford.

He stuck it in his backpack, and the motor started up nice and clean when he hit the button. He took Highway 41, just to feel the curves.

So, there. If she could see, she'd know he made good decisions. And if not . . . well, if not, he could see. He would know he didn't waste it, whether or not Mrs. Greenberg ever found out.

From *The Diary of Trevor*

Mary Anne and Arnie have never been very nice to me. Like when I told them I thought Clinton was gonna win the election. Arnie hooted and laughed at me. Bush, he said. George Bush. Bet on it. Mary Anne came to school the next day in a cap that said ROSS FOR BOSS on the front. "That's how much you know," she said.

Anyway, my mom said to pay them no mind. She told me a story of when she was a kid, and she told her uncle Bobby, who was this big football fan, that Joe Namath and the Jets were gonna beat the Colts in the Super Bowl. He laughed at her. Then, when the Jets won, he wouldn't talk about it with her. She said some people just can't handle being wrong.

I said, "The Jets and the Colts in the Super Bowl? Man. That must've been like a century ago. Both those teams are totally awful now."

"Thanks," she said. "Now I feel real old."

When I gotta get up and say my project flopped, Mary Anne and Arnie are gonna give me the business. I sure hope Clinton wins the election.

CHAPTER ELEVEN

Reuben

He stood in front of his first class, stomach unsettled and eye grainy from lack of sleep. "Today is the deadline for the extra-credit assignment. I'd like to see a show of hands. How many of you chose to participate?"

Mary Anne Telmin's hand shot up first, closely followed by another girl, named Jamie, who wore muted colors and tended to sit in the back and blend in with the walls. Then a boy named Jason, who liked to express his difficult growth phase by hitting and who needed all the extra credit he could get. After a second or two Arnie Jenkins raised his hand cautiously, the big, awkward, brutish boy who'd asked Reuben if he was a pirate.

"Chose to?" Arnie asked. "Or really did?"

"Did you participate, Arnie?"

"Well. I chose to. I could use the extra credit.

But I couldn't think of anything. I really tried, though."

"Hard to document trying, Arnie. I think you'd better put your hand down."

Reuben glanced at Trevor, who was staring at the wall on his right at close range. "Trevor?"

Trevor made a face and raised his hand.

"Is that it? Four? Out of a class of thirty-nine? Well, congratulations to the four of you for making the effort. Now. You documented your work on paper the way I asked you to? Would you pass those forward, please? Then we'll present the ideas to the class. Mary Anne, would you like to go first?"

She stood in front of the class as though she'd always known she belonged there and had never quite felt comfortable anywhere else. "Well, Earth only has just so many resources. So recycling is very important. And we don't have curbside recycling here in Atascadero. So I gathered some recycling bins, not enough for everybody in the city, of course, but enough for probably everybody who cares enough to ask for one. We put little ads on the bulletin boards around town, at the Lucky and the Kmart, saying we had them for free."

Reuben interrupted briefly. "We?"

"Oh. My father sort of drove me around. And

then I wrote a letter to the city council encouraging curbside recycling. And I got it signed by forty of my neighbors. There's a copy of the letter in with my paper, Mr. St. Clair."

"Thank you, Mary Anne. I'll take a look at that. What about you, Jason?"

Jason walked up the aisle slowly, pausing to kick another boy's foot. "Uh. Some people think we don't have gangs in Atascadero, but they're wrong. I mean, look at the graffiti. That's called 'tagging.'" He turned toward Reuben as he said this, as though everyone else in the room would know. "It's a kind of gang talk, like bragging. So I went to the store owners who got tagged and said if you pay for the paint, I'll paint over it. Some of it showed up again the next day, but I painted over it again. One store I did three times. But after a while I guess the taggers just got tired of doing it over."

"You wrote down all the businesses for me, Jason?"

"Yeah, it's all there, Mr. St. Clair."

"That's good, Jason. I'm impressed. Thank you." Not that the project was unusually impressive; it was more a consider-the-source observation.

Mary Anne Telmin seemed to get her nose out of joint when he said that, but truthfully, he had not been impressed by her project. Earlier in the semester it had become clear to Reuben that her father did most of the work. "Gathered" recycling bins, she'd said. Interesting euphemism for what a parent provides.

Trevor sat staring at the wall again. Reuben knew it would be a bad moment for Trevor, so he saved him for last, the way he might postpone his own pain if he'd had that choice.

"Jamie?"

Jamie shifted on her feet and stammered. "I went to the Oak Tree retirement home and talked to some of the people there. And a lot of what they told me, I wrote down. Like a story. Of their life. So the class could read about them. Because sometimes young people don't know that old people have a lot to say. If I could use the copy machine in the office, I could make one for everybody. I couldn't do it at the copy place, it would have been too expensive. It's almost twenty pages long."

"Thank you, Jamie. Why don't you talk to Principal Morgan during lunch today? See if she'll let you."

"Okay." She hurried back to her seat.

Reuben looked at Trevor and Trevor looked at him.

Trevor took a deep breath and trudged to the front of the classroom, moving slowly and warily, like he was walking a gangplank. Reuben felt his own face flush, as if the presentation, the pressure, were his own.

Trevor stood in front of the class and sighed. "I put a lot of time and energy into my project," he said. "But it didn't turn out like I wanted." Looking quiet and empty, he turned to the blackboard and sketched out a simple version of paying forward. He used Reuben's pointer to indicate the first circle.

"This was Jerry. I helped him get a job. But then he got arrested. I don't know why. I don't know if you can pay it forward in prison. I guess you can, 'cause I guess the people in there need a favor more than anybody. But I don't know if he will. Then, this was Mrs. Greenberg. I spent about three whole days fixing up her garden. Only, she died."

Arnie spoke out of turn, shouted out, "I wonder if you can pay it forward in heaven."

The class laughed and hooted, and Trevor exchanged a look with Reuben as though begging him to make it stop.

Reuben slammed his right hand on the desktop, hard. Trevor jumped. "Those of you who did not bother to participate will please stop making light of those who tried." The class stared at Reuben in stony silence, most with their mouths open. It was the first break in his calm evenhandedness, and Reuben knew by the looks on their faces that he'd just become the human equivalent of Lou's flying yardstick. "Please go on, Trevor."

"Oh. Okay. Well, there was a third one too. But. Well, I'm not quite sure how good an idea that was. Anyway, I'm gonna come up with three more people. You know. Start over."

Mary Anne Telmin raised her hand. "But, Mr. St. Clair, the deadline is past. He can't do anything about it now."

Trevor stiffened to her challenge. "I'm not doing it for the credit, Mary Anne. I'm doing it to see if the world really changes." He glanced at Reuben again for support, and Reuben gave him a subtle signal, pushing down with his hand as if to say, *Settle down. Don't rise to this.*

Arnie raised his hand and jumped in. "But you can't change the world on the honor system, anybody knows that. Leave people on the honor system, they don't do it. As soon as you look away, they just don't. I mean, look what happened."

Trevor rushed to his own defense again, tight

and bristly now, as if being attacked from every side. "It's not Mrs. Greenberg's fault that she died, Arnie."

"Well, people die, or they go to jail, or they just goof off, what's the difference? They still don't do it."

"All right. That's enough discussion. It's easy to stand here and criticize Trevor's idea because he had problems with the result, but it was still the best idea, especially since most of you didn't even have one. Now, I'll look these over tonight. Everybody who participated will see a positive effect on his or her grade."

But as Trevor returned to his desk and found his place in the textbook, the discussion continued in scattered whispers.

CHAPTER TWELVE

Arlene

She stood on his front porch with one hand poised to knock and her heart beating so hard, she could hear it in her ears. She hadn't done anything wrong, which was just exactly what she had stopped by to tell him, so why was she so afraid he'd tell her to get lost? Exactly when had this thing taken a wrong turn again?

She rapped hard on his front door and immediately wanted to run away. In fact, she'd taken two steps back when he opened the door.

"Arlene."

"Can I come in for just a minute?"

"Oh. Uh. It's a mess."

"Your place? Get serious. You're not the type to have a mess."

He opened the door just a little wider to show her the inside of his living room, all stacked with cardboard moving cartons. "I haven't quite unpacked yet."

"Well, Reuben. That ain't a mess. It's not your fault if all your stuff just got here, right?"

"Right," he said, still not sounding too sure of himself; but he stepped back from the doorway and let her in.

"Can I get you something to drink? I've got orange juice and ginger ale."

"Ginger ale'd be fine."

He went off to get it, and she sat chewing on the edge of her thumbnail, telling herself to stop it but not stopping. At least he hadn't told her to get lost.

When he handed her the cold glass, she said, "You never called me again after that movie. Did I do something wrong, Reuben? I have no idea."

He sat down beside her, perched on the edge of his seat the way he did whenever something made him uncomfortable. Well, see, he wasn't a total stranger. She knew that much about him.

"I'm not sure I can explain."

"Know what Trevor told me? He said you told him that it's better not to pretend like you didn't notice, because that doesn't fool you one bit anyway. And you know, when he said that, it made total sense. I thought, 'Shoot, I been doing it wrong all these years. I'm sure not going to make that mistake again.' So I didn't treat that side of your face like it didn't exist. So you left in a huff, and I ain't heard from you since."

"I'm sorry."

"You are?" She hadn't thought he would be; she'd thought somehow she'd come out sorry, the guilty one. That's the way it usually went. "Oh. Well, that's okay. Just kind of hurt my feelings some at the time."

"You're right," he said. "I get angry when people pretend they don't notice, and I get angry when I know they do. I'm not sure what I want from people. I think I want them not to jump a mile when they see me, and I'm never going to get that."

By that time she was crying, because she felt so bad for him. And for herself, truth be told. He didn't have any reaction to her tears, and she wondered if she wanted him to notice or if she wanted him to pretend not to. It was a hard problem, he was right about that.

Then he said, "Arlene, I've got a confession to make. These boxes didn't just arrive. They've been here for months. I just can't bring myself to unpack them. I've moved three times in the past four years.

I get so tired of it. Every time I try to unpack, I just get overwhelmed."

She stared at him and wiped tears out from under her eyes, sideways and carefully so she wouldn't smear her mascara. "That is so wonderful."

"What is?"

"That you told me that. That's the first real thing you ever told me about yourself. And I can totally relate to that. Not with moving, but heck, I feel that way about all kinds of things. I just get overwhelmed. Immobile, like."

And Reuben said, "Yeah, like that." And they smiled at each other and got embarrassed again.

"Maybe it would be easier if you weren't doing it alone. I could help you unpack."

"You'd do that?"

"Course I would. What're friends for? Just let me use your phone a minute, tell Trevor where I am."

Of course, the first thing Trevor asked was could he come over and help too, so Arlene put her hand over the phone and asked Reuben. Reuben said yes, of course, but additionally, he got this sweet look on his face, like he really liked Trevor, which Arlene already knew. But every time she saw it, she liked it better than the time before.

• • •

Trevor got deeply involved in a box of books. He arranged them on Reuben's bookshelf alphabetically, according to the name of the author. This seemed to impress Reuben, and it amazed Arlene, who knew he didn't get his knack for organization from her side of the family.

She stood in Reuben's kitchen unpacking better-than-everyday china, handing it up to Reuben, who arranged it on the high shelves. She felt so short beside him, like he was standing on a chair, which he was not. A little half-Siamese cat with blue eyes came mewing around her feet, and Arlene bent down to pet her. The cat arched her back and purred.

"I didn't know you had a cat."

"That's Miss Liza."

They hadn't said anything for a long time, and after saying that, they fell silent again.

The light through the windows went murky with a coming rain.

Then she opened the box with the pictures. They were all framed and laid flat, wrapped in newspapers. She unwrapped the top one. It was a photograph of a nice-looking young couple, a handsome young black man, hardly more than a boy, with his arm around a pretty girl. And the man looked a little familiar. Almost like Reuben.

When she looked up, he was over near the closet, looking back at her, watching her look.

"Is this your brother, Reuben?"

"I don't have a brother. That's me."

"Oh." *Boy, what a stupid thing to say, Arlene. "Oh."* But it was a shock, one she hadn't nearly adjusted to yet. She must have known, somewhere in the back of her mind, that he wasn't born with his face the way it was now. But she'd never thought about it, and certainly never expected to see what he'd looked like before, when he was still whole. So she just kept looking. And he just stood by the closet, watching her look. "Who's this pretty lady?"

"Eleanor. She was my fiancée at the time."

"But you never got married?"

"No. I've never been married."

Eleanor seemed about two shades darker in skin color than Reuben, smooth, shiny black skin, and her hair all drawn back, looking stylish, like somebody with a world of class. Like somebody Arlene never was and never could be. Like somebody Reuben really should be with. Arlene couldn't seem to get a bead on which face hurt her more. "I can't believe how handsome you were. Oh, no. I'm sorry, Reuben. Sometimes I say the stupidest things."

She looked over at Trevor, preoccupied with his bookshelf, to see if he was taking in any of this very personal stuff. He was not. He was lost in his own little world.

"Wouldn't it be nice if I still looked like that?"

"No."

She hadn't known she was going to say that. It just sort of said itself. And the funny thing was, he didn't ask her to explain. He just stuck his head in the closet and went on unpacking.

From *The Other Faces Behind the Movement*

Arlene

Because, you know, a man like that one in the picture, he would never have shown up in a little hick town like this one in the first place, and if he had, he'd be with that handsome, sophisticated woman, and I just know he would speak down to me.

It was real hard to stop staring at that picture. Hard to explain why. It felt like it had a hold of someplace in my gut and it wouldn't let me go. I mean, it just put a whole lot of things in a whole different light.

And then, when I got over that, there was the one of Reuben's parents. They were real good-looking

too. And they seemed to have that same something, that same thing Eleanor had, and I couldn't
even say for sure what it was, but this much I did
know: Reuben had it and I did not. He'd never
lose it and I'd never learn it. Some things start out
a certain way and never change.

After a while I set Reuben's parents down and
picked up that first picture again. While I stared
at it, I thought about my mother, and the way she
used to shop. We didn't have much money, see,
when I was growing up. So she'd buy seconds, different types of damaged goods, rather than an item
of clothing that was unflawed but poorer in quality.

"But, Momma," I'd complain, "it's got a stain on it."
And Momma would say, "Good thing for you it does,
little girl, or we'd a never been able to afford it."

Then I looked up at Reuben again, and he was
still standing in the closet, and one more time I
caught him looking back at me.

This hard rain started pounding on the roof.

She tucked her boy into bed at ten, since it was
Saturday and no school the following day. He asked if
they could get a cat and she avoided answering. A few
minutes into the eleven o'clock news came the knock.

The rain was really coming down. She didn't

115

even realize how much until she opened the door. It fell in sheets behind him, and he stood on her front porch soaking wet, his hair, his clothes saturated, water dripping off his chin.

"You're sopping wet. You better get in here." He stepped inside, and she closed the door behind him. "I'll get a towel."

She went into her bathroom to get the big cushy one. When she came out with it, he was standing by the couch, dripping water onto the carpet. She sat him down and toweled his closely cropped hair.

"Don't take this wrong, but what are you doing here?"

"I got lonely. It was the funniest thing. Something about having you and Trevor in the house with me all day. After you left, the house seemed so empty. I don't want to be alone anymore, Arlene."

"Why didn't you take your umbrella, silly?" She knew he had one. She'd unpacked it herself.

"I couldn't find it."

"I put it in your front closet."

"Oh. I didn't think of that."

"Doesn't everybody keep their umbrella in the closet?"

"No. I don't."

"Where do you keep it?"

"In the umbrella stand."

"What umbrella stand?"

"That tall wicker thing."

"Oh, is that what that was? I thought that was some kind of big, skinny planter. I put it on the back porch."

He said, "You seem tense."

"Do I?"

"Last time you were so sure."

"Yeah, well. Somebody had to be."

And then, listening to the rain on the roof, she was able to know what she should have known all along. What she *had* known all along in a very deep spot where she knew better than to allow herself to go. Alone, anyway.

That Ricky wasn't ever coming back.

And even if he ever did, what kind of woman would she be if she opened the door?

The handsome young man in the picture came back again, filling up her mind. She would never understand the forces that had brought him from there to here.

It took her back to that place again, the one she didn't like. The one where she knew that, by all rights, he was something she should never have been able to afford.

From *Those Who Knew Trevor Speak*

When I got home that night, I called Lou, long-distance. "Wow," Lou said. "You're seeing somebody. That's amazing. Wish I could say that."

I tried to explain that something felt dishonest about it. It wasn't easy to explain. The only examples I could find involved my shame in being seen by Trevor the following morning. He asked if Trevor seemed to mind, and I had to tell the truth and say no.

He pointed out that the only person who felt odd about it was me. I thought that meant I was worried about nothing. I'm used to that. It's a specialty of mine. That's what I wanted him to tell me, I think. That my anxiety was based on nothing, like a shadow with no mass behind it; then, once he'd told me so, I thought it would disappear like a shadow flooded with light.

That's not what he said. He said I was the only one who felt dishonest and I was the only one who knew my intentions. Maybe my intentions were dishonest.

I tried to dismiss his comment, but the minute he said it, I felt this great sweep of shame. I admitted to Lou something I'd never said out loud to anyone. Arlene wasn't quite what I'd pictured for myself. She wasn't someone I'd usher into a room on my arm with great pride.

"In other words," he said, "you're ashamed of her."

"I didn't say that."

"Sure you did."

All these thoughts started going around in my head at once, making it hard to breathe. I realized that this was her worst fear about me. That I looked down on her. Worst fears are always based on a grain of truth. That's what's so bad about them. I wondered if she had a friend she talked to like this. I wondered if she talked about my face and how hard it was to be physically close to me.

Lou said, "If you really want somebody else, go find somebody else. You're not doing her any favors."

I said, "No. I want her." It surprised us both.

I liked the way I felt around her. The way she made me feel. Which suddenly seemed so much more real and important than wearing a woman on your arm.

Lou told me a story about his most recent relationship. A man who, like most men in his life, held him at arm's length until Lou couldn't take it anymore.

"I finally issued an ultimatum. Get into my life, or get out of it. If you want to stop feeling dishonest, Reub, try making an honest woman out of her."

When I got off the phone, things began to look clearer.

CHAPTER THIRTEEN

Reuben

When he finally found it, the ring he knew was the right ring, he saw he would have to all but drain his savings, which he hated to do. Rainy-day money. It made him feel good just knowing it was there. But he knew it wouldn't be there for long.

The ring wasn't big enough to be flashy, but it was big enough, set in white gold with smaller diamonds halfway around the band. A little old-fashioned, but he liked that about it. A little like his mother's, but not enough to be significant. It was just the right one because he knew it was.

He left the ring sitting in the store, went home, and obsessed about it. Decided to sleep on it, but he didn't sleep well. In the morning he went by the jeweler's again, afraid it would be gone. When it wasn't, he put it on layaway, knowing he could still change his mind.

But at his next breakfast-table encounter with Trevor, he knew he had to do it. He looked at Trevor and knew. He couldn't buy a cheaper ring or cheapen their relationship by buying none at all. To do right by Arlene was to do right by Trevor. And, of course, himself.

He had it in his pocket the next night when he took her out to dinner.

She wore a rose-colored silk blouse and smiled openly, looking for all the world like someone he'd always known and always wanted to marry, with no doubts in between. He stuck his hand in his jacket pocket and grasped the little velvet-covered box. He was sure. He almost brought it out, but missed the moment. But he would. It was only a matter of timing. He was sure.

And she might not be.

He'd been so busy with his own doubts, he'd forgotten to consider the very real possibility that she might say no. He took his hand back from his pocket and tried to forget the box was there.

When he walked her to her door later that evening, they both claimed exhaustion. Reuben gave her a small, chaste kiss.

The moment made him nervous and reminded him of the moment she'd come into his home unexpectedly, right around the time he'd expected the kiss-off. He'd loved her for that. Even as he ran away. Everything else had been a game to avoid this very moment, when he knew that life with her was what he wanted, and knew also that something was wrong.

"You okay?" she said. Her voice sounded faint. Scared. Or he was scared enough himself to hear it that way.

"Sure. Why wouldn't I be?"

"I dunno. You seem kind of funny tonight."

"Just tired."

"Yeah. Me too."

He called himself a coward on the way to the car. Halfway home it hit him, like waking from a dream. He could not imagine what he had been thinking or why. He could not believe he'd almost said it out loud. He thought about Arlene, tried to bring her picture to mind, but she looked like a stranger. When he got home, he found the receipt for the ring in his drawer, right where he'd left it.

Miss Liza jumped on the bed with him and

rubbed against his chin. He told her everything. Described the cliff from which he'd almost jumped. She agreed that humans were impulsive and strange. At best. He told her he'd return the ring in the morning, but he never quite got around to that.

CHAPTER FOURTEEN

Matt

Matt was riding by an alley in Atascadero on his new motorcycle when he saw it. A man was sitting on the dark concrete in the alley, his back half up against a building, one arm wrapped around his own ribs, as if in pain.

Then the scene disappeared as the bike sped on.

Matt looked in his rearview mirror and made a careful U-turn. Drove back to the alley, turned in, and idled the bike down to a stop a few feet from the man's sprawled leg. He was young, maybe only a couple of years older than Matt. And his face was bleeding.

He looked up to Matt, eyes stony, but maybe with some fear hidden underneath. Matt didn't know who the guy might have expected to see, but it was clear by his face that Matt wasn't it. The eyes softened again.

"You okay, man?"

"Depends on your definition of okay. Been better."

"You need to get to a hospital?"

"No," he said. "No hospital. But I need to get somewhere that isn't here."

Matt woke at six the following morning, and the guy was still asleep on his couch.

He made a pot of coffee. He didn't have to work that day, which was good, because he didn't know this guy well enough to leave him alone in his apartment.

When the coffee began to drip, the smell seemed to bring his guest around.

"Good morning," Matt said. "I forgot what you said your name was."

"Sidney G."

"Right. I tried about ten times to talk you into going to the hospital last night, but you wouldn't budge. Seemed strange, but I figured you were delirious. But now it's morning, and you've had some sleep. And it's pretty obvious that arm is broken." He pointed to Sidney's right forearm, swollen to more than twice its normal size. "So you know you need an emergency room, right?"

Sidney G. sat up, defensively, Matt thought. "No, no hospital, man. Just a cup of coffee and I'll be on my way."

"Don't you even want to report what happened?"

"Report?"

"Yeah. Report. As in, to the police."

Matt watched the word register in Sidney's eyes. That's when he knew something was wrong.

"Nothing to report," he said, as if the whole thing meant nothing to him. But that made no sense. Then his eyes burned into Matt's. "Hey. Why'd you stop and help me, anyway? You don't know me."

"I was paying it forward. This lady who used to come into my store left me money in her will. She said I should pay the favor forward to three people."

"And then what?"

"And then they do the same." But Matt was increasingly sorry he'd ever brought it up. Because now he had doubts about this man he'd tried to help. And he wanted to take back what he'd said about Mrs. Greenberg's idea. He didn't want this guy's fingerprints on it. "You did something illegal, didn't you?"

"No, why would you say that?"

"Because you don't want a broken arm set, and you don't want to tell the police anything about who broke it."

"Nah, nothing like that, man. I'll just be going." Sidney G. rose unsteadily to his feet, then wobbled, as if he might pass out. He blinked, steadied himself. Headed for the door. "Don't worry. I'll do that . . . forward thing."

"No," Matt said. "Don't." His voice sounded cold and flat, even to him.

"Excuse me?"

"Don't pay it forward."

"Why not?"

"Because I think you did something illegal, and I think you're not who I thought you were, and I don't want you to be one of the three people I help anymore, and I don't want this idea in your hands."

Sidney G. moved close, until his nose was just a few inches from Matt's. Matt felt a cold clamp of fear in his gut, but he stood his ground.

"Well, well," Sidney G. said. "That's not very nice."

"You're welcome for bailing you out."

"Whatever, man." Sidney shook his head, broke away, and headed for the door.

Matt breathed a sigh of relief. "Wait," he said.

Sidney stopped. "Wait a minute." He walked into the kitchen and poured a cup of coffee into the mug he liked least. The one with the chip in the base. He looked up to see Sidney watching him curiously.

"Keep the mug," he said, carrying it to the door and handing it off.

Another strange moment of silence, Sidney studying his face for clues.

"But don't pay it forward."

"Right," Matt said. "I'll just find somebody else. Please don't."

As soon as the door closed, Matt called the Atascadero police to tell them what he knew; they thanked him for calling but told him the circumstances didn't match up with any crime. That they knew of.

From *The Diary of Trevor*

I have no idea what happened between Reuben and Mom. Must've been really weird, though. Because now every time I see Reuben, he says, "So. Trevor. How's your mom?" And then he says, "So. Does she ever ask about me?" *Ask what?* I'm always thinking. But it's usually better not to mix into these things.

Then I get home and Mom says, "Ever see Reuben?" And I say, "Yeah, I see him all the time." And she says, "So. Does he ever talk about me?"

Sometimes I want to yell at them both. I want to say, *Just talk to each other! It's not that hard! I mean, this is not brain surgery, guys.*

But grown-ups hate it when you talk to them like that. So I have this system. I never tell either one of them what they really want to know. Then, sooner or later, they're going to have to break down and talk to each other. Sometimes I worry that I'll be this weird about a girl when I grow up.

I hate to think that.

CHAPTER FIFTEEN

Arlene

Loretta stirred milk into her coffee cup with that little clink-clink sound that grated on Arlene's nerves. Loretta's Mr. Coffee machine was broken again, and since she had never been any too fond of instant, she had shown up at Arlene's house for coffee this morning. Arlene's Mr. Coffee machine never broke, so she was forced to conclude that Loretta used hers too hard.

Usually, she liked having Loretta around, the more the better, but she'd been out of sorts the past week.

Loretta's voice broke the stillness. "You don't talk much about him anymore."

"Who?"

"What do you mean, who? That guy you were all fired up about."

"Oh." Somehow she thought Loretta meant

Ricky, a fact she couldn't explain and chose not to mention. "I guess I been sort of avoiding him."

"So, what's the problem?"

"I wish I knew." She sat down, head in hands. This could not be delayed any longer. "Last time we went out, he was acting funny. You know how people act."

"No. I thought lots of different people acted lots of different ways."

"I mean how people act when they're trying to say something. Didn't you ever do that? Practice in the mirror, something you gotta say? And then, when you see them, it just sorta hangs there. Like everybody can hear it. I kept thinking the waiter could hear it."

"So, what did he say?"

"He never did. But I know anyway. He was trying to break up with me. I could tell."

"You don't know that until you ask him."

"I know now."

"You should ask him."

"Then he might tell me." She could see Trevor out the window, playing on the garage roof with his friend Joe. She'd never exactly told him not to, but he must have known she wouldn't like it all that well. When she stuck her head out the kitchen

132

window, he climbed back onto the plum tree and waved.

"So, you gotta talk to him sometime."

"I thought maybe I'd go over to his house with Trevor." That had worked out unexpectedly well last time, but it seemed a little tricky to explain, so she didn't try.

"So, now it's a big deal that he not break up with you."

"Why does that seem so strange?"

"Last I heard, you were just dating till Ricky came home."

Arlene rocked back in her chair and fixed Loretta with that look she reserved for the immature, the rude, and the plain stupid. "Ricky ain't comin' back. Don't you know that, Loretta?"

Loretta's eyebrows arched. "Don't *I* know that? Don't *I* know? Honey, on last count, the only living soul on the face of the planet to not know that was you."

Arlene sighed and threw the last of her coffee down the sink drain. "Well, I demanded a recount," she said.

When Trevor bounced through the kitchen door, she told Loretta to get lost. She said it in a kind of sign language—the kind that works only when you've known somebody a long time.

"I was just gonna have one more cup, Arlene."

Arlene picked up the Mr. Coffee machine, pulling the plug out of the wall as she carried it away from the counter. Three more cups' worth sloshed in the pot. "Be my guest," she said, and handed the whole mess to Loretta.

"Well. A brick wall don't have to fall on me." But darned if she didn't take the machine with her.

"Hi, Mom. How come you gave Loretta the coffee machine?"

"Oh, no special reason, honey. Listen. You ever see Mr. St. Clair now that school's out?"

"Sure, Mom. I see him all the time."

"Where, exactly?"

"I go over to his house."

"Oh. We should do that. Sometime. Together."

"Okay. Now?"

"Well. Maybe not now."

"Why not now?"

"We didn't call or anything."

"I never call. I just ride my bike over."

"Well, that's different, though, honey. With you."

134

"Why is it different?"

"Um. Give me a minute to think."

On their way over in the car, she asked yet again, "When you go over there, Trevor . . . and talk to him . . . does he ever . . . ask about me?"

"Yeah."

"How many times?"

"Every time."

"Really?"

"Yeah. Really."

"What does he ask?"

"He always says, 'How's your mother, Trevor?' and then I say, 'Oh, fine, she's fine,' and then he says, 'So. Trevor. Does she ever ask about me?'" A long silence. "If he asked you to marry him, would you?"

"He ain't gonna ask me that."

"If he did."

"He won't. Can we talk about something else?" It was time to change the subject anyway. It wasn't a very long drive.

When Reuben answered the door, Trevor bounced right in like he lived there. "Hi, Reuben," he called on his way by.

"Hi, Trevor. Arlene. This is a surprise."

He was in sweat clothes and unshaven. And he looked sad. Not that any of that mattered to Arlene, who was busy noticing how much she'd missed him. It was a big, heavy feeling, suddenly almost more than her insides could hold.

"Sorry I didn't call first, but—" *But what, Arlene? How you gonna finish that sentence? But I didn't want to give you a chance to say no? Don't bother.* Or worse yet, to hear him say her name in that awful way, the way someone does when they start a sentence that's going to hurt.

"It's okay. Come in."

She did, and she stood feeling awkward, aware of Trevor watching, not sure what to say. It wouldn't be like the last time, when they were unpacking and Trevor was all lost in another world. She wouldn't be able to really talk. But then again, she consoled herself, neither would he.

"Trevor, where do you get off calling Mr. St. Clair by his first name? I didn't raise you up like that."

"He said I could. Just for the summer. When I get back in his class in the fall, I gotta switch back."

"It's true, I said he could." Reuben agreed as he headed into the kitchen.

"Oh, you're in Reuben's class again next year?" Arlene asked, sounding both genuinely curious and optimistic, in about equal parts.

"Yeah. In a school my size, you know—there's only one social studies teacher for all grades."

"Well, that's great, honey."

Somewhere in the world, Arlene knew, there was something more to say. If she could only find it. She perched on Reuben's couch, and he brought her a ginger ale. The silence felt bigger than anything the house could contain.

Trevor said, "Where's Miss Liza?"

"I think she's out in the backyard, stalking birds."

"I'll go see." He thundered off, leaving Arlene with room to speak, which she now no longer wanted.

"Arlene, I—"

She jumped in fast, before he could say what she knew he would say if she wasn't careful. "I really missed you."

"You did?" He sounded surprised.

"Oh, yeah. Little things. I got used to having you around."

"What kind of little things?"

"Oh, just, you know." She knew he didn't.

"Like the funny messages you used to leave on my machine. I don't remember any word for word, but they were funny. I miss things like that."

"I'm sorry I didn't call. I've had a lot on my mind."

"Yeah. Me too." *Yeah. That's what they all say.*

She reached out and touched his right cheek. She was making a fool of herself, she knew, but she didn't care. She was almost ready to beg. Everybody regards that as so unthinkable, but somewhere in the back of her mind she figured people do it all the time. Just listen to popular music and you'll hear it. "I'd get down on my knees for you." . . . "Ain't too proud to beg." . . . "Baby, please don't go."

Before she could, Trevor came back in with the cat draped over his shoulder.

They stayed for an hour or so, during which Arlene spent most of the time marveling at the ease with which Reuben and Trevor talked to each other. She watched closely, like it was something she could learn.

The following night he called and asked her to dinner at his house. He said he was all settled in and felt ready to cook. "I was hoping to get your machine," he said. "I was going to leave a funny message."

"Want me to hang up so you can call back?"

"No, that's okay. I'll try to be funny when I see you."

That's when she first realized that he never had been funny before. Not face-to-face. Only as a voice on a tape.

"Reuben?"

"Yes?" She hated the way she'd said his name. That big, awful, weighty way that people do before bad news. She knew it came through that way too. Heard it in his voice. Everybody hates to hear their name spoken that way.

"The last time we went out?"

"Yes."

"I know what it was you were gonna say to me."

"You do?"

"Yeah, I do. But don't say it, okay? Please. Just don't."

"Okay. I won't." He sounded—she couldn't put her finger on it. Hurt? Relieved?

"You won't?"

"Not if you don't want me to."

Wow, she thought as she hung up the phone. *Who'd have thought it would be that easy?*

· · ·

The movie had ended, and Reuben's VCR had automatically rewound the cassette. She wasn't sure if he was asleep. She allowed herself to drift into a feeling, a sense, that she was somehow watching all this from above. Not so much physically, but more in terms of perspective. She'd been so sure it was over, but if she could have gotten up a little higher, seen a little farther, she might have been able to see this. She wondered if she would remember this feeling next time something seemed, in the short run, to be going wrong. She knew she probably would not. She knew people transcended that line of knowledge all the time, but darned if they didn't tend to cross right back again.

She whispered quietly, hoping to plant words in his head without waking him, without really calling attention to herself. "I'm so glad you decided not to break up with me."

His eye opened, and he blinked and swallowed as though he'd been half asleep. "Break up with you?"

"Yeah. But let's not even talk about that now."

"I was never going to break up with you."

"You weren't? Well, what were you gonna say to me, then?"

"Is that what you thought I was trying to say last time?"

"Yeah. It wasn't?"

"So that's what you asked me to please not say?"

"Yeah. What was it, then?"

She watched his chest rise with an intake of breath.

"Never mind. You wouldn't have liked it."

"Maybe not, but you sure know I gotta hear it now."

"Don't laugh, okay? I was going to ask you to marry me."

Arlene's throat felt tight. Even if she had known what to say, which she did not, she probably couldn't have said it. He braved the silence for a remarkable length of time.

Then he said, "Not right away. I just thought we could be engaged. For as long as it takes to get to know each other well enough. To take that step. I thought it might be better for Trevor. And better for you. Not in that order, though. I thought of you first. I thought you'd feel better wearing an engagement ring. Even if we didn't set a date right away. It was meant as a symbol of my intentions. Which are honorable. Are you ever going to say something?"

141

"You bought a ring?" That was something, probably as good a something as any other.

"I guess I did," he said. "Don't answer now. Just think about it."

She said she would. She didn't say she wouldn't think about anything else, that she'd be up all night thinking about it, but that's the way it turned out to be.

CHAPTER SIXTEEN

Reuben

Arlene had fixed chicken fajitas, Trevor's favorite, to honor the special occasion. Reuben ate too many, the way he had that first night in this house. The same house felt warmer now.

She had her hair done up, and she was wearing the ring on her left hand, but if Trevor had noticed, he'd failed to comment. Reuben figured he hadn't noticed. It wasn't like Trevor to fail to comment.

"Want me to clear the table, Mom?" Trevor said at last, breaking the quiet.

"In a minute, honey. Reuben and I have something we want to tell you."

"Okay, what?"

"I think Reuben wants to tell you."

"Okay. What?"

"Trevor? Your mother and I have made a big decision. One that affects you."

"Okay. What?"

"We've decided to be . . . engaged."

"Engaged? Like, to be married?"

"That's right." Reuben glanced over at Arlene, still holding her fork tightly, her eyes closed, as if the words might hurt.

"Yes!" Trevor shouted, startling Arlene's eyes open. "Yes! I knew it! I told you! This is so completely cool."

He jumped up from the table and launched into a little dance, which Arlene said made him look just like Deion Sanders.

Reuben said, "Who's Deion Sanders?"

He looked up to see both Arlene and Trevor staring with their mouths open. "Who's Deion Sanders?" Trevor asked, a study in astonishment. "You're kidding, right?"

Arlene rose to collect the dinner dishes, obviously more comfortable now that the tension had been broken. "Trevor, honey, not everybody follows football."

"Even so. Deion Sanders." He sat back down, elbows on the table. "Don't you ever watch football, Reuben? Hey, I just thought of something. Can I call you Dad now? Am I supposed to call you Dad?"

Reuben felt a little warm spot grow behind his

ribs, a place that for so long had known only pain. "That would be fine, Trevor. If you're comfortable with that. And if your mother is." Arlene looked at them both and nodded. "So, this Deion Sanders. Does he play for the Forty-Niners?"

Trevor rolled his eyes. "Boy. We got a lot of work to do on you."

"I thought Trevor was a Forty-Niners fan," Reuben said when she came back from tucking Trevor into bed.

"He is. But Deion Sanders plays for Atlanta. So he's sort of an Atlanta fan, too. When Atlanta plays San Francisco, he just can't handle it. He gets so upset, he can't even watch."

"I love you, Arlene."

The words seemed to reverberate in a suddenly empty room. Reuben wondered who was more amazed to hear them.

"We're gonna make a great family," she said after a time. "He sure loves you."

And then it dawned on Reuben, a thought he'd never had before. It was a sweet thought, but at the same time it stung somehow. He'd never quite known, or let himself know, how much he'd been missing by sealing himself so completely away from others. "I should go kiss him good night."

"Yeah. I think he'd like that."

Yeah. I think we both would.

From the chin down, Trevor lay covered in a Teenage Mutant Ninja Turtles bedspread. The light from the streetlamp showed the left side of the boy's face in a soft glow.

"Hey," Reuben said, and sat down on the edge of his bed.

"Hey." And then, as a pleasant afterthought, "Dad." A smile broke on Trevor's face and came all the way out of hiding. "Doesn't that sound cool?"

Reuben felt the contagion of the smile sneak onto his own face. "Very cool." They sat quietly for a minute.

"You know what? This means something went right with my project after all."

"I was thinking about that. About paying it forward. I was wondering how I'm going to do that. How do you do that, Trevor?"

"What do you mean? It's not a how, exactly. You just do."

"How do you think of things to do for people? I'm afraid I don't have your imagination."

"You don't think it up with imagination. You

just look around. Until you see somebody who needs something."

"That sounds easy." *Everybody needs something. How far would you have to look?*

"It *is* easy."

If you're a child, Reuben thought. "Good night, Trevor."

"Night, Dad. Is Mom happy?"

"I think so. I think we both are."

From *Those Who Knew Trevor Speak*

Actually, I think she was scared to death. But isn't everybody at a time like that, faced with such a big decision? I was scared to death too, but I had every intention of going through with it. But there was also . . . I mean, to complicate things for her . . . I mean, his name came up. Here and there. Which seemed normal to me. I still expected it would work out.

Until that day.

October 19, 1992. It's one of those dates you don't forget. In fact, you don't forget anything about it. You remember the jingle that was playing on the television. You remember the thought that was

147

spinning around in your head a split second before-hand, when everything was still in order. It's trite to say, but your life divides up into before and after, and you don't have trouble placing things in time anymore. You can almost date them, something like B.C. and A.D. I guess it sounds like I'm wasting a lot of time feeling sorry for myself. I won't lie. I haven't completely let go of it. In some ways I have. Not all ways. I'm probably being too sensitive. Maybe other people's wounds heal in a reasonable space of time.

No, I take that back. They don't.

CHAPTER SEVENTEEN

Reuben

October 19, 1992

Reuben sat on the couch sharing a bag of microwave popcorn with Trevor. Now and then, a piece fell, only to be retrieved by Miss Liza, who spent most of her time at Arlene's now, with the rest of the family. Every time she ate a kernel, Trevor told her that cats aren't supposed to like popcorn. She seemed unconcerned.

They watched Buffalo play the Raiders, a good game for Trevor to use as a teaching tool, since he wasn't overly concerned about the outcome. He cheered for Buffalo, but not so much that he couldn't breathe.

Just as the game had gone to commercial, Trevor had been attempting to teach Reuben the difference between a touchback and a safety. Also between a touchback after an end-zone interception and a touchback after a kickoff. Reuben

149

figured he had most of the basics down by now, but he might have been unclear on a few details.

A Coca-Cola commercial came on, the jingle familiar, destined to become too familiar, because now Reuben always thinks about it in connection with everything else. Not on purpose. He just hears it in his head every time the whole ordeal plays through again. Which it still does from time to time.

Trevor was feeding Miss Liza a piece of popcorn on purpose. She stood up on her hind legs to take it, one paw braced on Trevor's jeans, one poised in the air as if she might need to bat the prize away.

It should have been a good moment, a good day. A good life. By all rights, it should have been.

Reuben heard a knock on the door.

Arlene called in from the kitchen. Said she would get it. She swung the door open. Reuben looked up. Waited for her to say something. He couldn't see her face, just the back of her head, but he wanted to see her face for some reason.

A man stood in the doorway, saying nothing. A wiry, rather small man, with dark curly hair. The silence seemed to twist into Reuben's stomach somehow, as if stomachs can know things without needing to be taught. Reuben glanced over at Trevor, who stared at the doorway, his eyes fixed and expressionless. That cola jingle kept going against the back of Reuben's brain.

Somebody had to say something, and it was the stranger who finally spoke. "You don't seem too happy to see me." Then the wiry little man turned his attention to Trevor. "Aren't you even going to say hello?"

"Hello." Trevor's voice sounded hollow and cold. It never had before. That was the moment, really, that Reuben knew something had happened— something irreversible. Trevor never talked that way to anybody.

The man tilted his head. "You don't call me Daddy no more?"

CHAPTER EIGHTEEN

Chris

The call came in at seven a.m.; hard to think of it as a good thing.

Even through a fog of sleep, Chris recognized the voice immediately. Roger Meagan, a friend of sorts. A police officer he'd worked with while investigating stories.

"Sorry, Chris. I forgot you like to sleep in."

What he liked had nothing to do with it. He rarely got to bed until three. "What's up?"

"I'm not sure, really. I don't know. Maybe nothing. Maybe a story. I don't know. I guess that sounds stupid. Wake you out of a sound sleep, then say maybe it's nothing. But if it is something, it's something big. Real big. I just thought it might be a good thing for you to hear it first. I mean, it's known, but—one little angle of it. If you could break some pattern . . . if there is a pattern . . . oh, man. I'm not making much sense, am I?"

"You're sure not, Roger, slow down. Let me get my brain cells back in line. One fact at a time."

"You know gang killings have taken a real drop lately."

"I heard that. But it's just a fluke, right?"

"I don't know, Chris. I figure that's where a good investigative reporter comes in."

"So you want the name of a good one?"

"Shut up, man. You're good. You know you are. Look. Two months ago the number of shootings drops eighty percent."

"Drops *to* eighty percent?"

"No. *By* eighty percent."

"I didn't know it was that much."

"Well, everybody kind of wants to lay low about it. Like, you just know it can't last. Everybody acts like it's magic or something. We just stay real quiet, like we think we'll . . . I don't know, scare it away or something. Then last month, one death in all five city boroughs. One, Chris. Do you realize how remarkable that is? I mean, on a good weekend, sometimes we'd get two dozen. I mean, not a good weekend, but . . . you know."

"And this month?"

"Everybody's alive so far. So far as we know."

Chris felt his brain stretch. It was hard enough to try to figure out why things happen. But why they *don't* happen? It'd be like doing a story on the wind. What would he do, interview people on a street corner in the South Bronx? *Excuse me, ma'am, what's your theory on why you weren't hit by a stray bullet last month?*

"You think there's a reason?"

"Man, everything has a reason."

"Want to put your next paycheck on that?"

"There are no accidents in this world, Chris."

"Roger. Where on earth do you think I'd begin with something like this?"

"Start with a guy named Mitchell Scoggins. He knows something about something. We picked him up on a minor charge. Rumor is he went out to settle a score with some rival, but nobody got hurt. He said it was a point of honor. But—what honor? Whose honor? Since when is it a point of honor to go after your enemy and then not hurt him? It's like a new law on the street or something. But he won't tell me anything about it. I'm a cop. He's not going to talk to me."

"Where's Mitchell right now?"

"Doing thirty days at county."

1993 Interview by Chris Chandler, from
Tracking the Movement

MITCHELL: It's not a New York thing. I mean, now it is. But it didn't start here. It started in L.A. I mean, way I hear it. I mean, word on the street. They sayin' that.

CHRIS: I hear you know all about it. I hear the whole thing started with you.

MITCHELL: Nice try, man. You think I got a ego, huh? I tell you what the word is. Guy named Sidney G. He take credit for the whole thing. Tell you he the guy thought the whole thing up. Not that I ever met him. Sidney tell you all kinda stuff. That's the word on the street. Others say no. Sidney G. mighta got it started in L.A., but it's not his. Just picked it up somewheres. Brought it back.

CHRIS: What? Brought what back?

MITCHELL: The Movement.

CHRIS: This is all part of a movement?

MITCHELL: It moves, don't it?

CHRIS: Tell me about it.

MITCHELL: I don't know. I don't see how you one of us. I mean, who are you to me? Know when I'd tell you? If you crossed me. Then I'd come after you. But I wouldn't hurt you, not unless I'm all paid back. Forward, I mean. Then I'd say, "I come for you, but man, did you luck out." Then I would tell you. It'd be, like, part of my job.

CHRIS: What did you mean, "forward"? You said something about being all paid back, but you changed it to "forward."

MITCHELL: You need to go see Sidney G. He like to talk.

CHRIS: Know where I can find him?

MITCHELL: Nope. Never even met the man myself.

Looking for a man named Sidney G. Originator of the Movement. Want to make him famous. No personal questions asked. Or anybody else with info on Sidney G. or the Movement. Something about being "Paid Forward" or "Paying Forward." Write to C. Chandler at P.O. box below. Cash reward for right info.

He placed the ad to run for a month in the Los Angeles *Times,* then decided he'd wasted his money. Guys like Sidney G. don't read the *Times.* And he had no money to waste, because he'd done no real work for too long.

He visited his brother and borrowed another

grand, which was loaned with no guilt or bad feelings. He'd done it before and had always been good for it. Then he placed the same ad in the *Valley News* and the *L.A. Weekly*.

He got a P.O. box and tried to work on another story. Every day he checked the box. Every day it was empty. Not even crank letters from impostors out for reward money. Where would he get more money if something broke?

Dear C. Chandler,

Somebody I know see your ad in the Weekly and show it to me. Sidney G. didn't invent nothin. Not in his whole life. He used to be my boyfriend, but he is such a jerk. He got that thing from somebody he meet in Atascadero. He hide out there when things get hot. But it don't work forever.

Last I hear, his sorry self in jail. I don't know where or care. But his name ain't Sidney nor G.— that just what he call himself. His name Ronald Pollack Jr. No wonder you can't find him. I hope you got more trouble for him. I hope it's a trick. That's why I write this. Not for money. But I need money real bad. If you want to send some.

Yours truly,
Stella Brown

1993 Interview by Chris Chandler in Soledad State Prison, from *Tracking the Movement*

CHRIS: You could be a famous man. Right here in prison.

SIDNEY: See how much you know. I'm already famous in this prison. Legendary.

CHRIS: I mean famous all over the world. Could help your situation.

SIDNEY: In what way?

CHRIS: You know, go up before a parole board, and there it is on your record that you made this huge contribution to society.

SIDNEY: I don't even come up for parole till ninety-seven.

CHRIS: That could change too.

SIDNEY: What I gotta do?

CHRIS: Tell me how this Movement started.

SIDNEY: I told you. Started in my head.

CHRIS: You must be a really smart guy.

SIDNEY: I am.

CHRIS: How did you think of something this big?

SIDNEY: Just kinda come to me. I just saw the way things kept going all around me. I thought, "Somebody's gotta do something different. Change this mess." Then I thought it up.

CHRIS: Wow. I'm impressed. You didn't even hear or see something similar? You know, to put the idea in your head?

SIDNEY: Nobody put ideas in my head but me. So, how you gonna make me famous? I mean, even more than I already am.

CHRIS: Well, I produce freelance stories. I'll have to get a video camera in here. I'll have to go through channels for permission. Then, when we have a spot together, I can sell it to *Weekly News in Review*. They take almost everything I do.

SIDNEY: Maybe the governor'll pardon me. When he see it.

CHRIS: You're not exactly on death row, Sidney. I wouldn't count on a pardon. Maybe early parole.

SIDNEY: Yeah. Well. You do what you can for me, man. I'm sure you can see I don't belong here. Big contributions I could be makin' on the outside. The world need me out there.

CHRIS: Yeah. Absolutely, Sidney. I can see that.

Chris arrived back in his apartment in New York around seven a.m. Right away he called his cop friend, Roger Meagan, woke him up. That's justice.

"You did me a good one, buddy. I owe you. I

think this is going to be big. I don't know why I think that. No, I don't even think it. I know it. I just know somehow. Maybe it isn't big yet, but it will be. And by then it'll be my story. Not that I'm at the bottom of it yet. But I will be."

"Who'd you say this is?"

"It's Chris. Did I wake you?" He knew darn well he had.

"Chris, what are you talking about?"

"That story you put me onto."

"You got to the bottom of that?"

"I told you, not yet. But I will. Tracked it to this small-time convict calls himself Sidney G. He says he thought the whole thing up. He's full of it, of course."

"Thought what whole thing up?"

"The Movement."

"This is all part of a movement?"

"It moves, doesn't it?"

Roger groaned. "I don't know what it does, Chris. I haven't even had my morning coffee. Want to loan me some of your energy?"

I wish I could, he thought. He pulled off his shoes while he talked, the cordless phone clamped under his chin.

"It's like this, buddy. So far as I can tell. Somebody got it in their head to pass this thing along. It's like a pyramid scheme, only it never goes back to the originators. People just keep doing amazingly nice things for people, and it just keeps going forward. It never goes back."

"So what's the angle?"

"There doesn't seem to be one. That's why I'm so excited about this, Roger. Thing is, it's a bear to track down, because, apparently, there are no names involved. People go around saving lives, sparing lives, giving money away, and most of them never know who it was that helped them. No records kept."

He'd learned more about this last part from his visit to Stella than his interview with Sidney G. Sidney had remained sketchy on details. Stella had looked at the five one-hundred-dollar bills in his hand and opened right up.

"That's weird, Chris. This is weird."

"You bet it's weird. That's why I love it."

"But, Chris. I mean . . . if somebody saved your life, wouldn't you get their name? So you could pay them back? You know, what goes around comes around?"

"But you never pay it back. You always pay it forward. Like, what goes around goes around even faster."

"That makes no sense."

"Why doesn't it?"

"What good is it to the person who started it?"

"Well, this is the world they have to live in. Right?"

A long silence on the line. "So this lawbreaker is real altruistic?"

"No. I told you. He's full of it."

"So who started it?"

"I don't know. But I'm going to find out. I'm going to do a major puff piece on this fool. On *Weekly News in Review*. Make him out to be a total hero. Then I'll put out some kind of eight-hundred number or P.O. box or something, for people with more information. This thing must have touched a lot of people's lives by now."

"Chris. If the guy's full of it, why do you want to make him out a hero?"

"Because he's a liar, Roger. And somebody out there knows it. Somebody out there might take offense when they get a whiff of his attitude. Might want to set the record straight."

"Sounds like career suicide. You'll come out the fool."

"Anybody can be taken in, Roger. My career'll survive."

"It's a long shot, Chris."

"Life is a long shot, Roger."

He hung up the phone. It would work. It had to work.

From *The Diary of Trevor*

It feels like there's something wrong with not liking your own father. Like I should be ashamed about that. But it's true, and I don't know what I'm supposed to do about it.

Yesterday I said that to my mom. That I just don't like him. I thought I might feel better to say it out loud.

I thought she would yell at me or hit me or send me to my room.

Instead, she just looked tired.

CHAPTER NINETEEN

Arlene

She bumped into Reuben one Saturday morning at a gas station on the Camino. She hadn't seen him in months. She didn't see his white Volkswagen until after she'd gotten out of her car, and when she did, she almost got back in and drove away.

Her heart got to pounding so bad, she could hear it in her ears. She felt dizzy and strange and couldn't decide what to do.

And then he came walking out of the convenience store and saw her. He turned his gaze down to the asphalt and headed toward her, toward his car. She could tell he wanted to walk the other way—that showed—but she was parked close to his car, so there was no way out for either one of them.

"Reuben," she said, thinking her voice sounded scared. He didn't look up. He didn't say anything. She could still hear her heart. "Reuben, say something, okay? Yell at me or something. Please?"

He looked up. She met his eye. It made her dizzy again. He looked away.

"Reuben, I just had to try, you know? I had to. Thirteen years, Reuben. He's the boy's daddy and all. Scream at me and tell me I hurt you and I'm not even fit to live, 'cause I know it's all true. But don't just stand there and say nothing."

He walked around the pump island, right up to where she stood. The toes of their shoes almost touched. He looked deadly calm. She looked at his face, so close up like that, and it struck her that she'd missed him. Struck her so hard, it almost knocked her down.

"He's the biological father," Reuben said. She'd never heard his voice like that before. Deep. Scary, almost. "In what other way has he been a daddy to that boy?"

"Well, that's just it, don't you see? He wants to make up for that now. He wants to pay back what he took from me."

Reuben turned away. He walked to his car and drove off without looking back.

When she got home, Ricky was lying on the couch, watching TV.

"You moved any muscle at all since I left you?"

"I don't need a lecture today," he said. He barely moved a muscle to say it.

"Thought you was gonna look for work."

"On Saturday?"

"Any old day would do. And if you ain't gonna do that, at least pick up your clothes and do your own stinky dishes."

He swung around and sat up slowly, like it hurt him to do it. "What got into you this morning? I ain't never heard so many complaints come out of you all at one time."

"I been saving 'em up."

"Thought I told you I didn't need no lecture." It came out so loud, so strong and angry, she wouldn't dare say anything else. Which she guessed was probably the point. "What got into you? Huh, Arlene? You hear me talkin' to you? Can't I do anything right anymore?"

"I dunno, Ricky. Can you?"

Then she stood, without backing off, and blinked too much, waiting to see what he would do. He didn't explode the way she expected. Just brought his hand up to his face and rubbed his eyes, like the whole thing made him feel tired. She watched his face and wondered why she used to think he was so handsome. He wasn't, really—at least, not taken one feature at a time.

She looked up to see Trevor standing in the kitchen doorway. "I thought you were playing outside."

"No, I was in my room."

He turned and slipped away again. She followed him down the hall and into his bedroom.

"Trevor, honey? I'm sorry you had to hear that." She waited for him to say something back, but the waiting hurt, so she couldn't do it for very long. "I ran into Reuben this morning."

"Oh, yeah?" But it was said with little emotion.

"I thought you'd be interested in that."

"I see him at school all the time."

"Oh. Right. Does he ever ask about me?"

"No." That's all he said, just "no." Kind of flat and cold. He didn't go on to say, *Why should he?* But Arlene could hear it anyway; she could feel that place in the air between them that those words didn't fill.

"Honey, I know I made a mistake."

"So fix it."

"I don't think you understand, Trevor." Tears took hold against her will. They felt hot and angry. She could think of all kinds of things he wouldn't understand, including some she didn't understand herself. Like why she wasn't ready to give Ricky the boot, even as bad as things were going. She chose to state the one reason that lay completely out of her hands, the part she could not change if she tried.

"Reuben's real upset, honey. He got hurt. No matter what I said to him, he wouldn't take me back now. No way. You didn't see him this morning, honey. He's never gonna forgive me."

"You don't know that he wouldn't."

"I know."

"You don't know until you ask him."

"I know now."

"You should ask him."

"I can't, Trevor."

"Why not?"

"He'd say no."

"So? You could ask."

"See, honey. You don't understand. Like I said. I guess it's a grown-up thing."

She looked over her shoulder on the way out of his room. Trevor looked down, picking nervously at the bedspread.

"Maybe I don't want to be a grown-up, then."

"Well, honey, nobody really does. Heaven knows it got shoved on me against my will."

She closed the door quietly behind her.

When she got out to the living room, the TV was still blaring, but no Ricky. His GTO was missing from the driveway. The dirty dishes and clothes were all still there.

That same evening Arlene was sitting on the couch watching TV with Trevor. Watching that program called *Weekly News in Review*—which she never found all that fascinating, anyway—and her thoughts ran elsewhere.

She pulled her attention back to the program. Trevor said, "This might be interesting."

"What might? I missed what he said."

"Next story coming up is about how gang violence might be about to become a thing of the past. Because, like, one person came up with an idea to change everything."

"I'm sorry. I forgot to pay attention."

"That's like what I was trying to do. Only not with gangs. Just, you know. One person changing everything."

By now the program had gone to commercial.

Arlene heard the loud, unmuffled motor of Ricky's GTO in the driveway. Her heart jumped.

She reached for the remote control and shut

off the TV. "Go on into your room now, honey."

"I wanted to watch this program."

"I'm sorry, honey. This is important. I gotta have a private talk with your daddy."

He left the room like he'd been told.

When Ricky swung the door open, she could tell he'd been drinking. He was trying to hide it. Maybe that's how she could tell. He was trying too hard to hide it.

"We need to talk, Ricky."

"Not now, hon. I'm gonna take a hot shower."

"That's good. You do that."

While he did, she packed up all his belongings, which really wasn't much, and loaded them into his GTO. She left him one pair of jeans, one shirt, and one pair of socks, which she laid out on the bath-room sink.

Ricky dressed and left with no words spoken and, remarkably, no trouble.

From *The Diary of Trevor*

I saw this weird thing on the news a couple of days ago. This little kid over in England who has this, like . . . condition. Nothing hurts him. Every time they showed a shot of him, he was wearing a crash helmet and elbow pads and knee pads. 'Cause I guess he would hurt himself. I mean, why wouldn't he? How would he know?

First I thought, *Whoa. Lucky.* But then I wasn't sure.

When I was little, I asked my mom why we have pain. Like, what's it for? She said it's so we don't stand around with our hands on a hot stove. She said it's to teach us. But she said by the time the pain kicks in, it's pretty much too late, and that's what parents are here for. And that's what she's here for. To teach me. So I don't touch the hot stove in the first place.

Sometimes I think my mom has that condition too. Only, on the inside, where nobody sees it but me and maybe her friend Loretta. Except I know she hurts. But she still has her hand on that hot stove. On the inside, I mean. And I don't think they make helmets or pads for stuff like that.

I wish I could teach her.

CHAPTER TWENTY

Chris

The 800 number rang directly into his home. And rang and rang. It rang in the middle of the night, jarring him out of sleep. Most wanted more information about the show they'd seen earlier that night. Nobody seemed to have information. Everybody seemed to want it.

At six in the morning he gave up, drank a pot of coffee, and watched the phone. It didn't ring for hours.

At ten after nine the phone rang again.

The caller said, "I want to talk to someone who's responsible for that stupid news program last night."

"Well," Chris said, "the thing is, you are."

He listened to a silence on the line. "Oh. I am?"

"Yes. You are. My name is Chris Chandler, and I wrote, produced, researched, and otherwise put that story together."

"Well, it was a piece of garbage, man."

"Everybody's a critic."

"I can't believe you bought those lies about that guy. Sidney G. Man. He is such a jerk. He's a total liar. How could you have bought all that trash?"

"Actually, I didn't."

"You didn't?"

"No."

"You didn't believe he thought up that whole thing?"

"No."

"Then why did you run that stupid story?"

"Well, it's like this. I know he's a liar, but what good does it do to say so? I got nothing to go by. I don't really know. I was hoping somebody who actually knows something would help me call him a liar."

Chris did not feel inclined to believe he had such a person on the line or, suddenly, that he likely ever would.

"Well, I know something, and I say he's a liar."

"You know where he got this idea?"

"Yeah. He got it from me."

Oh, right, kid. I see. It's not all Sidney G.'s idea. He's just a lying jerk. You thought the whole thing up. You deserve all the credit. "Okay. So you're the real hero, and I should do a show about you?"

"No, I didn't think it up. I just paid it forward. I just found Sidney G. in an alley in Atascadero, and I tried to help him. I told him about the Movement."

Chris felt a little tingle behind his ears. Atascadero. Stella had said Sidney hid out in Atascadero when things got too hot. But he hadn't mentioned that in the story, because he didn't want Sidney to know he'd ever talked to her.

"Uh. You know . . . what's your name?"

"Matt."

"Matt. I'm sorry, Matt, if I was being a little rude. All night I've been up talking to people who know less than I do about all this. So, listen, you don't happen to know how this thing got started, do you?"

"Only that it didn't start with that Sidney G."

"And you don't know who it was that paid it forward to you?"

"Well, yeah. Of course I know that. Her name was Ida Greenberg."

"Wait. Wait just a second, okay, Matt? I have to get a pen. I have to get a whole lot of information before you hang up. Don't hang up, okay?"

When he got back with the pen, just before he wrote down the information, Chris said, "One more thing I don't get. If this Sidney G. is such a jerk and a liar, which I agree he is, why did he pay it forward? But I don't know why I'm asking you. You probably don't know."

"I got a theory."

"Let's hear it."

"Because I told him not to."

"You think he did it because you told him not to."

"Yeah. I said I didn't want him to touch it. My theory is, nobody tells Sidney G. what he can and can't touch."

Chris sat baking for a moment at the curb. Atascadero was hot, unbelievably hot. The guy who rented him the Ford said this was unseasonable, like that should somehow help. Chris had rented the Fairmont at the San Luis Obispo airport. It felt boxy and strange, like something his father would drive. It did not have air-conditioning.

He checked the address again, the one that Mrs. Greenberg's neighbor had given him. It was all the way across town from Mrs. Greenberg's home. Supposedly the address of a son, the sole surviving heir. He shut down the engine and walked up to the door.

He knocked. Waited. Knocked.

He heard the sound of a small, high-revving

engine, like a power mower. He couldn't tell if it was coming from the backyard of this house or the house next door.

He walked around to the back and looked over the ancient wood fence. A man in his forties was cutting the grass. He wore a sleeveless white T-shirt and tight jeans.

Chris already didn't like him.

He didn't seem like a man who would keep an obsessively neat garden, but that's what Chris saw. Flower beds covered in chips, roses trimmed and tied back. Not one blade of crabgrass on the lawn. Seemed this guy could tend his yard but not himself.

Chris called hello a few times but couldn't make himself heard over the roar. He leaned on the fence and waited, feeling sweat creep down the nape of his neck and run down his back.

When the man finally saw Chris out of the corner of his eye and looked up, Chris waved his arms. The man stopped and cut the motor, leaving just a humming echo in Chris's ears and a welcome silence.

"I'm looking for Richard Greenberg. Would you happen to be him?"

"What'd'ya want?"

"I just wanted to ask you a few questions about your late mother."

Richard snorted. "Not exactly my favorite topic."

"Why's that?"

"I got my reasons."

"Because she didn't leave you anything?"

"What do you know about that? Hey, who are you, anyway? You some kind of friend of hers? Yeah, all right. She stiffed me when she died. You know that much. Left me one dollar. Left the rest of her life insurance to these people she hardly knew. That's what kind of swell lady my mother was. What do you want to know and why?"

"That's what I wanted to talk about. Her will. What about her house? Did she own it?"

"Her and the bank. She left me in the cold, I'll tell you. One lousy dollar. Now I gotta live over this guy's garage and do his garden so's he'll gimme a break on the rent. Which is kind of ironic. Because I think the reason she stiffed me was that she got mad at me 'cause I didn't do her garden. I figure this is, like, Ida's revenge. What exactly is your stake in this?"

"I'm just a reporter looking into a story. It seems she was passing on some kind of . . . I'm not sure how to explain it. Like a chain letter, but with deeds instead of letters."

"I don't know nothing about that. I got no idea why she did it." He turned quickly and started back to his mower.

Chris reached into his pocket and pulled out the photocopy Matt had made for him. The letter. "I'll tell you why she said she did it."

Richard turned back. "Said to who?"

"One of the people she left the money to."

He moved closer again. "That crazy cat lady?"

"No. The kid from the grocery store."

"Oh, right. That was so rich. What a slap in the face. I been her son for over forty years. These two little teenage strangers bag her groceries and they get my money."

He ripped the photocopy out of Chris's hand. Chris watched him read silently for a few seconds.

"'I don't trust that he would use it the right way.' That's a good one. I would have invested it in eating. That's such a lie. She was mad about the garden." He threw the letter up into the air. The pages fluttered onto the still-uncut grass. "I said I'd do it. She finally paid some kid to. Said she didn't pay him—he did it for free. Yeah, right. Kids love to do that. She was obsessed with that garden. She never loved me that much. I gotta finish here." He walked away from the fence again.

"Excuse me. Can I have my letter back?"

Richard ignored him and pulled the string on the lawn mower; the noisy engine jumped to life. Chris pulled himself up to the top of the fence and scrambled over, rescuing the letter just before Richard could run it through the shredder.

"Did you talk to the lady at the cat shelter?" Terri asked.

"Yeah. She really didn't know Mrs. Greenberg at all."

"I really didn't, either. I just ran her groceries over the scanner." Terri stood in the alley behind the grocery store.

Chris squatted with his back up against the building, his eyes closed against the heat and glare. A light breeze had come up, and even the breeze felt hot.

"I don't know," she said. "I wish I could help you."

"Did you talk at all when she came in?"

"Barely. She usually complained about her arthritis. She was nice, though. I make her sound like she wasn't. But she was. Nobody likes to listen to someone complain about aches and pains. But I figured she had to tell somebody. You know? She was lonely. Her husband died. So I listened. Now I'm glad I did. I mean, for eight thousand dollars she could have told me about every ache she ever had."

"Do you remember the last time you saw her?"

"Kind of. She was in a good mood."

"What did she say?"

Terri let her head drop back and closed her eyes. She shook her head. "It was such a long time ago. You know?"

"Okay. I understand. Look, I'm staying at the Motel 6. Maybe another day, maybe two. I don't know. Maybe I'm wasting my time and I should go home. But if you think of anything. If anything comes back to you. Give me a call, okay? And if you think of something later . . ." He handed her one of his cards.

She slipped it into her shirt pocket. "I guess my break's over. Sorry I wasn't much help."

"You were as much help as anyone else," he said, and walked back to his rented oven.

He found her house. That was easy. The tricky part was explaining to himself why he was even bothering. A dead woman's house wasn't likely to tell much of a story.

The sun had dipped to a slant, the day's heat broken, but barely. He stood in front of the little blue-gray house and admired the garden. Perfectly tended. Someone new must be living here now.

He knocked on the door; no reply.

He sank onto the top porch step and began to feel stuck. His motivation to leave drained away. He could go get dinner, but he wasn't hungry. Why go back to the motel when he wouldn't sleep?

A boy rode down the street on a heavy old bike, delivering the afternoon paper. He didn't throw one at Mrs. Greenberg's house. Maybe the bank still owned it. But banks don't keep up the yard work. Do they? Maybe whoever lived here didn't take the afternoon paper.

Chris took his MasterCard out of his shirt pocket and stared at it. Tapped it on his knee. He'd used it for a plane ticket and a motel and a rental car. And for what?

A woman came out of the house across the street to fetch her paper. Chris sprang to his feet.

"Excuse me," he called, and sprinted over. It seemed to alarm her. "Excuse me, can I just ask you a question about this house across the street?"

"Old Mrs. Greenberg's house?"

"Right. Did you know her well?"

"Not very." She crossed her arms, uncrossed them, tugged at her housedress nervously. "My husband doesn't think we should get too friendly with the neighbors."

"Is someone living in the house now?"

"No, it hasn't been sold yet. The bank owns it."

"Who's keeping it up so nicely?"

"I really couldn't say. If you'll excuse me."

She backed inside and closed the door quickly. Chris took a deep breath and walked back to Mrs. Greenberg's front porch. He stood looking through the front windows. Sheets covered the furniture. Everything seemed coated with a fine layer of dust. He collapsed on her steps again.

He should just go home. He knew that now. He couldn't interview a dead woman, and even if he could, where would it lead him? Someone paid it forward to her. Maybe she didn't know that person's name. Maybe she was part of the twelfth generation, or the hundred and twelfth. If he was the best investigative reporter on the whole planet, and he wasn't, he could never trace it all the way back to its roots. Not without some kind of written record.

The paperboy came back and dropped his bike

on Mrs. Greenberg's perfect lawn. He came up the walk toward Chris. Chris waited, figuring the kid was heading for him or had something to say to him, but he took a detour around to the side yard. As he walked by, Chris saw he was carrying a bag of dry cat food.

When he came back, he had a pair of hedge clippers.

"Hi," Chris said as he walked by.

"Hi." The boy began trimming the hedge that ran like a fence against the neighboring property. It wasn't looking too seedy to begin with.

When he'd worked his way closer, Chris said, "You're the one keeping this place up."

"Yeah."

"Who pays you to do it?"

"Nobody."

"Why do you do it, then?"

"I don't know. Just because." He furrowed his brow and concentrated on his work for a moment. Then he looked up and said, "I don't think she would like to see it get all ratty again. I don't know if she can see. What do you think?"

"About what?"

"Do you think that when somebody's dead they can still look down like that?"

Chris wrestled with the question for a moment, then shook his head. He'd never really pinned down what he believed in that respect. "I guess not. But I'm not sure."

"No, I'm not sure either. I figured it's better to be safe."

"So, you knew her."

"Yeah."

"Did you know her well?"

The boy stopped his work, let the clippers hang straight down from one hand, and scratched his nose with the other. "Not real well, I guess. We used to talk."

"About what?"

"Oh, I don't know. Stuff. Football. This project I was doing for school. She was gonna help me with this project. But then she died."

Chris rose to leave. He could talk to every living human in this city and not stumble on anyone who really knew. But he had to try one more time, because in the morning, he now knew, he'd be flying home.

"You wouldn't happen to know anything about her will?"

"Her what?"

"Her will. Why she left money to certain people."

"Oh. That kind of will. No. I didn't even know she had a will."

"Yeah. I didn't figure you would. Well, goodbye."

"See ya."

Chris sat in the car for a few minutes, watching the boy work. Thinking it was odd for a boy that age to work for free when he had death as the perfect excuse to get out of it.

Then he wondered if Mrs. Greenberg was looking down. *If you are,* he thought, *how about a clue? How about letting me see something here?*

But all he saw was a boy cutting a hedge. He started the motor and drove away.

From *The Diary of Trevor*

I don't think even one single person has paid it forward.

I guess it was a stupid idea. A bunch of people said it was stupid, but mostly just the people I think are stupid, like Arnie and Mary Anne and a couple of other kids in class. And Joe, who's my friend, but he didn't say it was stupid. He didn't say anything. But he had that look on his face like he didn't get it. So maybe he thought it was stupid, but he was just too nice to say so.

Anyway, they were right and I was wrong. Nobody did it.

Only, I think Mrs. Greenberg would have. If she could. And Reuben wants to. I know he does. But he just can't think of anything that big.

Here's the part nobody seems to get. It doesn't even have to be that big. I mean, not really. I mean, it might just seem big. Depending on who you do it for.

CHAPTER TWENTY-ONE

Reuben

Reuben arrived home from school at four fifteen. Trevor knocked on his door at four thirty.

"Where's Miss Liza?"

"In the kitchen eating. I just fed her. Is that why you came by, Trevor? To see the cat? Or did you want to discuss something?"

"That second thing." Reuben stepped back and swung the door wide. Trevor came in and perched on the couch. "If you don't mind."

Of course he minded, considering the possible topics. "Of course not, Trevor. You know you're always welcome here."

Miss Liza came running in from the kitchen and jumped on Trevor's lap. "Wow. She must've heard my voice, huh?"

"You should be flattered, Trevor. You're more important to her than food."

While he small-talked, Reuben nursed a sinking feeling in his chest, familiar but more pronounced than usual. He'd thought he would still have Trevor, could always be friends with Trevor, but it hadn't worked out quite that way. It hurt to have the boy around, and Trevor seemed to notice. Trevor's once-daily trips to Reuben's house had dwindled. The last time, he'd claimed he'd only come to visit the cat, and he hadn't stayed long.

"What's on your mind, Trevor?"

"I was just wondering if you were still going to pay it forward. I guess you don't exactly have to. The way it worked out. I just thought maybe. I just wondered."

Reuben took a deep breath and sank into his chair. Sometimes, when the urge to cry came around, and it did, it seemed to come behind both eyes, like an ancient trace memory.

"I've thought about that, Trevor. I guess I still would, if I could. I just don't know yet, what I could do for anybody. I'm having a hard time with that."

"I know somebody who needs something."

"Is it someone I know?"

"Yeah. My mom."

"I'm sure your dad can help her, whatever it is."

"He's gone again. She told him to go. Besides,

he couldn't have helped her with this. This is something nobody else could do except you."

Reuben's chest burned. She'd told him to go. Did that make everything better, or worse? "Look. Trevor. I really respect the work you did on that project. And I'm going to do my part to keep it going. Sometime. With somebody. But the way things stand between your mother and me . . ."

"Yeah, that's what she said. She said you were upset. But I thought, that makes it really good, you know? Because it's supposed to be a big something. You know. A big help. And if you help somebody you really want to help, then that's not very big. You know? But if you're all mad at my mom and you helped her, that would be a big thing." His fingers scratched behind both of Miss Liza's ears, and she leaned in closer and purred, her eyes half closed.

Reuben stood and walked to the window, needing to be as close as possible to somewhere else. As if through a long tunnel, he heard himself say, "I'm sorry, Trevor. I'm not sure I'm a big enough man to do something like that."

Trevor's face twisted with disappointment. The cat jumped off his lap and ran back to the kitchen. "Don't you even wanna know what it is that she needs?"

"Maybe it would be better if we just talked about something else."

Trevor shrugged. "I got nothing else I was gonna say."

"Tell me more about what you said earlier. You said she told him to go."

He shrugged again. "Not much to tell. They kept fighting. Couple days ago she told him to get out. And he did. I guess I'll go home now."

"I'll give you a ride."

"Nah. I got my bike out there."

"I don't mind. We'll put it on my bike rack."

"I guess. I gotta go say good-bye to Miss Liza."

They rode to Arlene's house in silence.

Why had he suggested driving the boy home? Reuben asked himself that question all the way there. If he really didn't want to see her, and he really didn't, why hadn't he just let Trevor pedal home the way he always had?

He wanted to ask Trevor if his mother was home or at work, just to prepare himself, but he couldn't quite bring himself to say the words.

He pulled up across the street. Her car wasn't parked out front. A wash of relief and disappointment struck, warring, with Reuben as the unfortunate battleground.

He cut the motor, and they sat quietly for a minute, listening to an odd, intermittent crashing sound, like a series of small car accidents. It seemed to be coming from nearby.

"I wonder what that is," Reuben said absently. He didn't feel particularly motivated to drive away again.

"I'll see." Trevor got out of the car, leaving the passenger door open, and walked a few paces. He stopped opposite his own driveway with his hands in his pockets. Then he came back and sat down in the car beside Reuben.

"It's my mom. She's pounding the heck out of that truck with a baseball bat."

A wave of cold numbness struck deep in Reuben's gut. His ear began to ring again, and this time he could hear his own blood rushing around in his head, like the ocean in a conch shell.

"I thought she wasn't home."

"No. She's home."

"Her car's not here."

"It broke down. Now she has to take a bus to work. I think that's why she's all mad at the truck. She still has to pay for it. And now she's gotta take a bus to two jobs. She had to go back to the Laser Lounge nights."

"Since she threw your dad out?"

"No. All along. He never really made much money or anything." The ugly metallic sounds of her pounding punctuated their words and their silences. "That's my baseball bat too. Man. That thing's never gonna be the same."

I wish I could do that, Reuben thought. It made him feel itchy and explosive, feeling how much he had to vent.

"Did you want me to get her a new car, is that it?"

"No. That wasn't it."

"You wanted me to give her rides home from work at three in the morning? I guess that is a dangerous time to ride the bus."

"I don't think the buses even run that late. No, Harry the waiter drives her home."

Pound. Pound. Always the give of metal. No breaking glass. Reuben tried to remember if the truck still even had glass. "What, then?"

"What, what?" Trevor seemed distracted by the noise too.

"What does your mother need that only I can do?"

"For you to give her another chance. She knows

she really messed up. She knows that now. She does that a lot. You know, like, sees a good thing and a bad thing and takes the bad one. She's not dumb. She knows. I don't know why she does it if she knows. It's just this thing she does. She says you'll never forgive her. But I figured, well, you could. It would be a really big thing. But you could. If you wanted to do a really big thing. For somebody. I mean, I remember you asked me once how you do something really big like that. Remember? And I said, well, you just look around. And find some-body who needs something. So, she does. Need something. I just thought you'd want to know."

The interior of the car rang with the absence of words. The pounding continued outside. Reuben could hear Trevor's breathing. He wanted to hug the boy because he missed him, but nothing moved. "I'm sorry, Trevor. I can't."

"Okay."

"I'm sorry."

"Okay. She said you'd say that."

"You talked about this with her?"

"Not exactly. She just said you were upset and you wouldn't ever forgive her. But I said she should ask. But she won't, 'cause she knows you'll just say no. So I asked."

"I'm sorry, Trevor."

"Okay. Whatever."

The pounding stopped suddenly. The unfamiliar silence felt strange and stunning.

Trevor got out of the car without saying goodbye. He took his bike down and walked it across the street. Reuben waited and watched until Trevor closed the front door behind him. He started up the engine.

As he cruised by the mouth of the driveway, he braked slightly. He didn't tell his foot to do that, but it did.

Arlene stood with the bat on her shoulder, panting and sweaty. She looked up and saw him immediately. The bat clattered onto the driveway.

Reuben pushed the accelerator to the floor. The little engine sagged, then picked up. In his rearview mirror he saw her standing in the middle of the street.

He heard her shout his name. "Reuben. Reuben, wait."

He swung around a corner, though it would have been more direct to go straight.

CHAPTER TWENTY-TWO

Arlene

Trevor had gone to Joe's on a sleepover. Arlene sat home alone, thinking how she'd like to drive by Reuben's. Maybe she'd get her courage up, even knock on the door. For three weeks she'd been wanting to do this, and probably would have done it. If she'd had a car.

Now it was her night off, and she'd finally saved up enough money to fix the old Dodge Dart. So it stood to reason she should take a drive, right?

A light burned in Reuben's bedroom, and his car was parked out front. She circled the block and drove by again.

On the third trip she stopped and cut the engine and just sat awhile. Looking. Thinking about a time when she was welcome there and could have knocked and gone right in. Thinking about how the cat used to rub up under her chin and how they would have been married by now and could have pooled their financial resources to get her a new car. He would have helped, she knew he would. That was just the kind of man he was.

Something big and heavy sat in her chest. It felt harder and harder to breathe around it.

Her heart pounding in her ears, she walked around to his back door and knocked. The back door opened, and Reuben stood in the doorway in his bathrobe. He didn't look angry. Big and imposing, that he looked. And yet at the same time vulnerable somehow, like he couldn't really make her go away, even if she were to physically drive home.

"I thought you were just going to sit out there all night," he said.

"You knew I was out there?"

"Of course I did. You left Trevor home alone?"

"He's spending the night at a friend's."

"Oh." He slid his hands into the pockets of his robe, and they stood a moment, both looking down at the stoop. "Why the back door?" he asked after a time.

But that was a question she couldn't answer. If called upon to guess, she might say it had something to do with shame, but she wasn't anxious to learn exactly what. So she changed the subject as best she could.

"I love you, Reuben." She allowed the words to echo between them until their sting wore off. She hoped he would say something, maybe even something nice. But she could wait only just so long. "I guess that's all I came by to say. I know it doesn't really change what happened. But I wanted you to know. I don't guess I ever said that before. Even though it was true enough. Anyway, I just had to say it now."

His hands came out of his pockets to hang at his sides, and his chin rose slightly. "I notice you didn't feel compelled to say that until it was over with him." His hand came up to the edge of the door, leading her to believe she'd better talk fast, before it slammed shut.

"That's not why, though, Reuben. I know it looks that way, but it's not. Know why? It's because of that time you drove Trevor home. And you went by the driveway and slowed down. Almost stopped. Until then, I thought you just flat out wouldn't talk to me. After that I knew part of you wanted to talk to me and part of you didn't." She winced slightly, waiting for the door to slam, but his hand found its way down to his side again. "I know you don't forgive me, Reuben. I don't expect you to. But some little part of you must miss me, right? Heaven knows I miss you."

She reached for his dangling right hand, and he allowed it to be held. He looked into her face for a minute, even though it seemed to hurt him. The light wasn't good, coming mostly from behind him, and she wasn't sure of her ability to read his face. She smiled, hoping he could see, hoping she was not about to cry.

Then his hand disappeared again.

"Don't, okay? Just go home now, Arlene."

She could hear in his voice that he was crying, and it startled her. He'd never cried before, so far as she knew. It was a weakness she attributed only to herself. She knew he would want no witness. So she did as she had been asked.

CHAPTER TWENTY-THREE

Chris

He hadn't been home long, and he was still exhausted. So when the phone rang, he almost let it go. Almost.

"Hello?"

"Chris Chandler?"

"Yeah. Who's this?"

"Terri, from the grocery store. You know. From Atascadero? Am I catching you at a bad time?"

"Uh, no, it's fine, Terri. What's up?"

"Well, you said to call you if I thought of anything. Only this probably isn't much. It's probably nothing. But I did think of something. That last time I saw her? I remember what she was in such a good mood about. I remember I said her garden looked really nice. And her face just lit up. And she said, 'Oh, isn't it wonderful?' or something like that.

She said, 'The neighbor boy did all that.' She told me his name, but I forget it now."

Chris waited in silence a moment, hoping for, expecting, something more. Her garden had been important to her. That much he already knew.

"Well, I said it was probably nothing."

"No, I'm glad you called, Terri. Really. If you think of anything else . . ."

"Well, that's it, I guess. Just that she was all happy about the garden."

"I appreciate your calling, Terri. I really do."

"Well, I don't want to run up my phone bill. Bye."

Chris hung up the phone, blinking slowly. It came in through the back of his mind, in the unwelcome voice of Richard Greenberg. Three sentences, echoing: "Said she didn't pay him, he did it for free. Yeah, right. Kids love to do that."

Richard was right. She paid a kid to do her garden. She must have. Which had no bearing on this situation whatever. Useless. So she was happy because her garden had just been done. It meant nothing. But he couldn't let it go. "Said she didn't pay him, he did it for free." Big favor, for a kid. For anybody. What kind of kid would do that for free?

And then he knew. Something magical in the revelation, because he'd asked Mrs. Greenberg for a sign. *Let me see something.* And all the while he'd been looking right at it. What kind of kid would do that for free? Same kind of kid who would keep doing it for free long after the lady was dead.

He'd been looking at the next link back, and he'd driven away.

He shouldn't have asked the kid if he knew about her will. What a stupid way to go at it. Why would the kid know about her will? Nobody knows how someone else is going to pay it forward. He should have asked the paperboy if he knew anything about the Movement.

"The paperboy," he said out loud.

He sat on Mrs. Greenberg's front porch. The weather hadn't changed, or if it had, it had changed back to hot in his honor. The neighbor lady across the street glanced out her kitchen window now and then, as though she'd do well to keep an eye on him. *Imagine how crazy she'd think I am,* he thought, *if she knew I'd come three thousand miles to sit here. Twice.*

A paperboy came by, on foot, walking the route

with a cloth bag over his shoulder. A red-haired boy with freckles. He lobbed a paper at the house next door.

"Hey, kid." The kid froze, looked panicked. Didn't answer. "I don't bite."

"I'm not supposed to talk to strangers."

"I just want to know what happened to the other kid."

"What other kid?"

"The paperboy who was here last month."

"He won the prize."

"What prize?"

"Best paperboy of the year. He won the week off with pay."

Oh. Chris thought of the nearly maxed MasterCard in his shirt pocket. It wouldn't keep him here another week. The red-haired boy was trying to hurry past. "What's his name, do you know?"

"Trevor."

"Trevor what?"

"I forget." Level with Mrs. Greenberg's walkway, the boy broke into a run and disappeared down the street.

Chris began walking in the opposite direction. Passing the next-door neighbor's lawn, he briefly picked up their paper. The *Atascadero News-Press*. He memorized the street number of their office, on the main drag. El Camino Real.

He found the newspaper office, sold them a song and dance about a national award for enterprising young people. They gave him a name and address without question. He got lost twice trying to find it, finally had to stop for gas and a map.

When he knocked on the door, it was after ten a.m. It wasn't until the sound of his knock faded that Chris felt awake enough to realize that the kid would not be home. Kids go to school on weekdays.

A small, pretty, dark-haired woman flew out the door. "I'm twenty minutes late for work. Whatever you're selling, I ain't buying it." She pushed past him into the driveway and stood beside an old Dodge Dart, fumbled in her purse—for keys, he assumed. The car was parked behind a late-model truck, stripped, and damaged as though it had been through a meteor shower.

"Shoot," the woman said. "Left my keys in the house."

"What happened to that truck? Looks like somebody took a lead pipe to it."

The woman turned the knob on her front door, then ran into it, as though amazed that it didn't open.

"Shoot. I locked myself out." She turned to consider him, as if for the first time. "Who are you and why aren't you going away?"

"My name is Chris Chandler. I'm a reporter. I'm looking for Trevor McKinney."

"He's at school. Where did you think he'd be? And I'm late for work and locked out, and standing here talking to you ain't puttin' me in no better mood."

"Did you leave any windows open?"

"Just that high one."

"Come on. I'll give you a leg up."

He laced his fingers and offered his hands like a stirrup, poised under what he assumed to be the bathroom window. She stepped up onto his hands, surprisingly light. She reached up to the window, put her fingers under the screen, and pulled hard, bending the frame. The screen shot across the driveway, mangled, he presumed, beyond repair.

She leaned the top half of her body through the window, and he hoisted her up higher. She disappeared.

A moment later she came barreling out the front door again.

"So where's Trevor's school?"

"I'm late for work."

"You'd have been a lot later if I wasn't here."

"I wouldn't have locked myself out if you hadn't distracted me at the last minute."

"Where's that school again?"

"What do you want with my son?"

"Just want to ask him a couple of questions. About a Mrs. Greenberg."

"I don't know no Mrs. Greenberg."

"He does."

"For all I know, you could be a kidnapper. I gotta go."

She drove off without so much as a wave good-bye, cutting a little close to his legs on the way out of the driveway.

As it turned out, there was only one junior high school in town anyway.

Chris stopped at the office, where he was given a visitor's pass and instructions to room 203, where Trevor McKinney was apparently scheduled to arrive for social studies class.

When he stepped into the classroom, only the teacher was present. Chris stared at the teacher's face for a protracted moment, then glanced away. He felt he needed to look more closely but didn't dare.

"Chris Chandler," he said, and stepped forward to shake the teacher's hand, focusing awkwardly on his tie. "I'm looking for a Trevor McKinney. I was told he'd be here next period." He flashed his visitor's pass.

"Yes. Take a seat, Mr. Chandler."

The teacher seemed curious but asked no questions.

Chris glanced at the teacher's face again, and the man looked up, as if he could tell. Chris turned his eyes to the blackboard as though he'd planned to all along. The board was blank, freshly erased, except for a sentence in neat block lettering:

THINK OF AN IDEA FOR WORLD CHANGE AND PUT IT INTO ACTION

"Is that an assignment?"

"Yes."

"Interesting assignment."

"It can be."

"Any of the students change the world yet?"

"Not yet. Some of them had good ideas. Trevor had a particularly good one."

Three students walked in and slapped books down on desktops. Chris recognized the paperboy immediately. The boy looked back at him.

"Remember me?" Chris said.

"I think so."

"From Mrs. Greenberg's house."

"Oh, yeah."

The boy walked over and stood by his desk. "I think I asked you the wrong question," Chris said. "So now what I'm going to ask is this: Did somebody do a big favor for you, and is that why you take care of Mrs. Greenberg's garden for free?"

"No. Nobody did a big favor for me."

"You don't know anything about the Movement?"

The boy's face looked blank. "The what?"

Chris felt something sink in his gut. Another expensive trip to nowhere. Another dead end. What good would it have done anyway? So the boy might have taken him one link back. Then it all falls down again.

He stood to leave.

"Well, bye," Trevor said.

Chris shifted his weight from one foot to the other and back again. "Your teacher told me you had an interesting idea for that assignment." He pointed to the blackboard. The room was filling up with children now, a claustrophobic feeling.

"Yeah, I invented this thing called 'paying it

forward.' It was for last year's class. I got the best grade. But you know what? It was a total bust."

That tingle hit behind Chris's ears, a hot feeling, slightly dizzy. He smiled. "Maybe it didn't work out as bad as you thought," he said.

From *The Diary of Trevor*

There are absolutely no words for how cool this is.

First off, everybody's telling my mom what a great mom she is. And everybody's telling Reuben what a great teacher he is.

And then they're saying I'm a great kid, and I say, "Nah. Not really."

I mean, anybody could have thought of this. It's so simple. Sometimes I think, *How could it work? That's so amazing.* And other times I think, *How could it not work? It's so simple.*

The part about believing people might really do it. I bet that's the part nobody could get right before now.

But you know what? If they want to tell me I'm brilliant and special, let 'em.

It makes Mom and Reuben happy.

CHAPTER TWENTY-FOUR

Arlene

Y ou taping this, Mom?"

Arlene was not only taping, but counting the number of times he asked. "Yes, Trevor, like I told you the last six times." But there was no genuine impatience in her words. She understood.

"I think we need more chips, Mom."

Arlene sighed. Normally, she'd have told him to get up and get more chips himself, his hands weren't broken. But his grandma was here, having driven all the way from Redlands to share this moment. And Joe and Loretta and Ricky's sister Evelyn, the boy's aunt, were here. And Reuben was a maybe, though he hadn't shown yet. And it was an irreplaceable, special moment for the boy, Trevor's very own moment, so Arlene supposed she could understand how he didn't want to miss even a minute of the program. Even though it was going on tape. Even though Chris had promised him a professionally taped version of the segment. Even though the segment hadn't begun yet and everybody was staring in endless, nervous fascination at a story about welfare reform that would have bored them to tears on any other night.

She brought a fresh bag of chips out from the kitchen, and the show went to commercial. Arlene pushed the long, ribbony hanging strings of a few helium balloons out of her way to wade through bodies to the VCR.

"Don't turn it off!" Trevor shouted, and everyone jumped.

"You want the commercials?"

"Maybe they'll come back and say something about the next story."

"Okay, fine. I ain't touching it." She raised her hands in an exaggerated surrender.

She went back to the kitchen for another iced tea for her momma and a 7UP for Loretta. She pulled back the kitchen curtain, staring down the empty street as if she might see him drive up. Maybe he was just running a little late, she thought. Even though he'd never been late to anything in his life, so far as Arlene knew.

Then she heard it from the living room. A

narrator talking about Sidney G. and the story they'd done before. How a bit more information had come to light. How pleased they thought the viewers would be to see the real thinker behind this wave of kindness that threatened to take over the country with sudden goodwill.

And then they said Trevor's name. It made her stomach tingle. Trevor's name on national TV. *My son,* she thought, and her knees felt a little too wobbly to move back into the living room. Just for a moment she wondered if it was really fair to call him her son, even though he was, because it felt like taking credit for his sudden fame. Really, she did not feel the least bit accountable. By all rights, any son of hers should have been an average kid, and she supposed in most ways Trevor was. Which is what made all this so odd and amazing.

"Mom, get in here, quick! It's on!"

She wobbled into the living room with little help from those knees. On the small screen Trevor was riding his bike down Mrs. Greenberg's street, throwing newspapers onto the lawns. Trevor. Her boy. The same one who sat on the couch in twitching silence, watching. Arlene tried to remember if she had ever known anyone who had been on television, but no one came to mind.

That old bike looked so shabby. She'd have to get him a new one. Why hadn't she already? What would people think?

She leaned both hands on the back of the couch, and her momma reached back to put a hand on Arlene's. Gave it a squeeze and then left it there. It was such a strange moment, she almost forgot to watch the show. But it was on tape anyway, and she'd probably have to watch it four or five times before it all sank in properly. Her momma's hand on hers. For once in Arlene's whole life, she must've done something worthy.

Now Trevor was standing in the yard beside Mrs. Greenberg's house, showing where he keeps the dry cat food that he buys with his own money, because he knows Mrs. Greenberg wouldn't want any of those strays to miss a meal in her absence. And the power lawn mower he uses to keep her grass neat, even though it isn't really hers anymore. And the plastic gas can he has to tie to the handlebars of his bike when the mower runs out of gas. And most of this was unfamiliar to her. She was learning, along with much of the country, what her son did while out of the house. He had a life, and it hadn't struck her before, at least not in such an obvious way, that he existed on his own, apart from her.

Now the inside of a classroom. Her gut constricted at the image of Reuben in front of his blackboard. In front of that sentence. The one that started it all.

She reached across the couch and gave Trevor a little nudge on the shoulder. "Did he say he'd come?"

"Huh?"

"Reuben."

"He said he'd try."

Suddenly, Arlene felt the need to drive by his house, to see if he was sitting home, watching alone, to avoid her company. But it didn't seem right to duck out of the festivities. Not on Trevor's big night.

Maybe Reuben would arrive in time for the postprogram celebration.

Reuben did not arrive, though. Arlene brought out more dip and waited for a moment alone with Trevor, so she could tell him how proud she was. But the company stayed, and the program got shown three more times, with Trevor fast-forwarding through the commercials. With all the excitement, Trevor was asleep long before that moment could present itself for real.

• • •

She woke in the morning when Trevor came in to kiss her good-bye. His grandma was ready to drive him to school.

"You too big a celebrity to ride your bike now?"

"Aw, Mom. She just wants to."

"We'll get you a better bike real soon."

He sat on the edge of the bed, and she parted his hair with her fingers and brushed it aside.

"One I got's okay."

"Nah, you deserve better."

"Love you, Mom."

"I'm real proud of you, Trevor. Just so proud, I could split. Know that thing about how everybody gets fifteen minutes of fame? That's just about how much time they gave you on that show, huh?"

"School today's gonna be real fun. I bet Mary Anne Telmin won't even talk to me." His face twisted into a satisfied smile. "Mom?" he said on his way out the bedroom door. "I like my bike okay. Really."

Then he blew her a kiss.

When she got home from work the next day, her momma was gone. But she'd left a note by the phone in that distressingly perfect penmanship of hers.

That reporter fella called. Really needs to talk to you. He wants to fly out and see you in person. Something concerning Trevor, and some mail, and something I didn't quite get, only that it was about the White House in some regard. Call him collect if you want. As soon as you can.

Love,
Momma

Arlene took a deep breath and picked up the phone. She didn't feel right calling Chris collect. It would have made her feel poor, like a beggar. The phone rang five times, then his answering machine picked up.

"This is Chris Chandler," the machine said. "If this is Arlene McKinney, I'm on my way to the airport to grab a red-eye to California. I'm sorry to catch you off guard, but we really need to talk in person. All kinds of stuff going on. I promised you I wouldn't give out your address and phone number, but now I've got all these important messages for you. They want me to start the interviews for the Citizen of the Month spot right away. You have no idea how much timing is involved with this. This story may not stay hot for long. See you in the morning. If it's anybody else, please leave a message." *Beep.*

Arlene glanced at the clock and wondered how long Trevor's fifteen minutes of fame was destined to last.

The knock came before eight a.m. Arlene lay very still and listened to Trevor's footsteps running to answer the door.

By the time she'd managed to dress herself and get out to the living room, Trevor had nearly buried himself in a mountain of envelopes, tearing them open like a kid unwrapping Christmas presents.

Chris stood when she entered the room, but she waved him down again.

"Look, Mom. I got four hundred and nineteen letters. And that's just the first two days. And not only that, but Chris says the network wants to tape an interview with me for Citizen of the Month. You know that thing they do on the six o'clock news? Well, next month it's me. I'm going to be the Citizen of the Month! Cool, huh? Chris'll tell you all about it. And that's not even the best part. I get to go to the White House! The president invited me. To meet him. Me!"

Trevor stopped and gasped for breath. Arlene

wanted to shake herself more fully awake. Probably some parts of this were happening and other, less likely parts were not.

"The White House?"

"Yeah! Cool, huh?"

"*The* White House?"

"Yeah, the president wants to meet me. And Chris says it's gonna be on all the news shows and in all the papers. Me shaking hands with the president!"

Arlene looked away from Trevor's breathless expression to Chris. "All by himself?" she asked Chris, who opened his mouth to respond but never got a word in edgewise.

"No, Mom, you get to go too, on account of you're my mother, and Reuben's invited too, because he was the teacher who got us to do that assignment in the first place. All expenses paid. We get to stay at the Washington Arms Hotel. And Chris says somebody from the White House is going to come get us at the airport in a big car and tour us around the city. Isn't that just totally cool?"

"You and me and Reuben?"

"Yeah, isn't that just totally cool?"

Out of the corner of her eye Arlene saw Chris smile shyly. A trip to Washington with Reuben.

Who she couldn't even bring herself to call, to ask if he'd seen himself on TV.

"That's pretty cool, all right, Trevor." She tried to sound sincere. Because it was cool, unbelievably so, to the point that it hadn't all quite settled in yet. But with Reuben . . .

"Remember when you said we're all supposed to get fifteen minutes to be famous? Chris says I'm gonna get, like, hours. Boy, I better start answering some of this mail."

From *The Diary of Trevor*

Well, this is the last I'll get to write in this diary for a while. 'Cause I am leaving it home. Shoot, I got a president to meet. I won't have time to write in a silly diary.

But, boy. When I get back. Watch out.

Reuben says I have the rest of my life to write down everything that's about to happen to me.

Is it bad that mostly what I'm thinking is that Mary Anne and Arnie and Jason and Jamie and Joe will be jealous of me? I hope not. Because that's one of those things you just can't make yourself unfeel.

CHAPTER TWENTY-FIVE

Reuben

In the airport Trevor talked to him. And talked and talked. Endless strings of breathy speculation. What the president would be like, what sights they would get to see. Would they have to go through a metal detector or show ID to get in?

He asked Reuben several times, in several different ways, if Reuben thought his Citizen of the Month interviews had gone okay. Then he showcased his knowledge of White House history.

"Did you know there was a fire there?"

"I think I might have heard that."

"That's why they painted it white."

Reuben thought Arlene was not listening, but she broke in on that comment. "You're making that up."

"No, really. The War of 1812. And in 1929. I think they painted it that first time. Is it okay to call him Bill?"

"Who?" Arlene asked absently.

"The president."

"Oh, my heavens, no! Don't you dare. Don't even think about it. You call him Mr. Clinton, or President Clinton, or Mr. President, or just plain 'sir.'"

"What if I get to meet Chelsea?"

"Cross that bridge when we come to it."

"I hope I get to meet Chelsea. She's a major babe."

On the plane Trevor opted for the window, and Arlene sat next to him, which put Reuben on the aisle, beside her. It seemed awkward not to talk, but he didn't.

Trevor looked out the window, and Reuben fingered the little ring box in his pocket and wondered again why he'd brought it. And wondered, if she knew he'd brought it, would she then understand that his silence wasn't cold, or wasn't meant to be, but rather a trench he'd dug himself into? A trench that seemed to only deepen with his movements. Maybe at some point in the trip he would tell her, just so she would know that for a moment, while packing, he had missed her, and his thoughts had been kind.

But that was a big bite for a man who couldn't even seem to discuss the weather or their itinerary.

The flight was a smooth one, so he read his book.

At the airport a very young, fresh-faced man in a suit and tie held a sign that read MCKINNEY PARTY. The man, whose name was Frank, loaded their luggage in the trunk of a black American-made car and asked if they'd like to stop at the hotel to freshen up. Arlene said that sounded good, but Trevor looked so crestfallen, they asked what he'd like to do first.

"See things."

"Well, that's my job today," Frank said. "To show the three of you around, get you safely back to your hotel, and then I'll be back to get you tomorrow morning at nine o'clock sharp. We'll take a little tour of the White House until it's time for your appointment with the president."

"What do we see first?" Trevor said. He and Frank seemed to have formed an instant bond, cutting Reuben and Arlene out of the loop. Which was as it should be, Reuben felt, because this was Trevor's day.

"What all do you want to see?"

"The Washington Monument, the Library of

Congress, the Jefferson Memorial, the Lincoln Memorial, the Smithsonian . . ."

"We might not get to all those today," Frank said. "But there's tomorrow afternoon. What's first?"

"The Vietnam Memorial."

Reuben flinched unexpectedly at the mention of the name.

Walking down the Mall, approaching the Vietnam Veterans Memorial, Frank dropped back and addressed Reuben by name.

"I understand you're a vet."

"I am."

"I'm not going to give the usual tour guide spiel. I've noticed that vets don't always like that. You probably know a lot I don't. You might want a moment to view this by yourself."

Reuben swallowed past a tight knot in his throat. Until Frank reminded him, he'd avoided focusing on the depths of his own discomfort.

Trevor said, "We'll wait back here for you a minute, Reuben, and Frank can give me the tour guide spiel. I wasn't there."

Frank's polite laughter rang in Reuben's ears as he walked toward the Wall. The sound of his own footsteps seemed to echo, bigger than life. Seven weeks in Vietnam. Then a week to stabilize in a medical installation and a quick flight to a stateside hospital. The men with names carved into this black granite had known something about the war. Reuben knew only what he saw in the mirror every morning. Maybe, he thought, that was enough.

He studied the index for a time, looking for a specific name. Then he moved along the Wall until he found the correct panel, reflecting a time late in the war, and ran his fingers across the names until he found Artie's. It jolted him slightly to see it, the reality of it, a recurrent nightmare suddenly become provably real. He reached up and traced the letters with his fingers.

A minute or an hour later he felt Trevor at his right side. In that sudden moment of the child's presence, Reuben knew that his wounded pride was harming Trevor as much as or more than Arlene, and causing Reuben to sacrifice far too much in its name.

"Reuben, do you know how many names there are here?"

"About fifty-eight thousand, I think." It felt strange to talk, and he realized he hadn't for quite a while.

"Fifty-eight thousand one hundred and eighty-three. Who's Arthur B. Levin?"

"An old buddy of mine."

Arlene's voice startled him from behind. "Trevor, maybe Reuben wants to be by himself."

"No, it's okay, Arlene, really."

"Maybe he doesn't want to talk about Arthur Levin."

"No, it's okay. He was just someone I got to know in basic training. Artie was the guy voted most likely to mess something up." He wasn't sure if he was telling this to Trevor, or Arlene, or both. "First time Artie pulled the pin on a grenade, his hands were shaking so much, he dropped the grenade. Into high grass. Stood there digging around like he could find it to throw it. I knew he'd never get it in time. He was going to blow himself away. So I ran in and grabbed him, tried to get him to clear the area. Too late, though."

"He died?" The quiet voice of Trevor.

"Yes."

"Did you get hurt, Reuben?"

"Can't you tell?" A silence. "I didn't even know him that well. Just better than anyone else there. He was the only person on the continent who wasn't a total stranger." He felt Arlene's arms circle his waist from behind. "Sometimes I look in the mirror and think, 'What if I had just run? Just saved myself.'

Artie would be just as dead. And I'd still look like the man in the picture. Just a little older." But looking at the Wall, he had to wonder: What if it hadn't happened and he hadn't been sent home? Would he be a name carved in granite now?

Arlene's breath tickled his ear. "That's not the kind of guy you are. Besides, you'd always wonder. If you could've helped."

"Whereas this way I know I couldn't. Trevor? Go talk to Frank for a minute."

"Okay, Reuben."

Reuben turned and held Arlene. Neither said anything for a few minutes.

He took a big breath. "I've been doing a lot of thinking, Arlene. I'm the kind of person, when I finally let myself love someone, it just goes so deep. You know what I mean? I know you do. Because you're the same way. So I was thinking. Maybe I can understand that loyalty you felt."

"What do you mean?" From the sound of her voice, he figured she knew but couldn't quite believe he meant it.

"What happened with Ricky. Maybe I should feel lucky to have a woman like that. Because, years from now, when we have that same kind of history, I know I'll get the same level of loyalty from you."

"You saying what I think you're saying?"

He placed the little velvet box in her hand. "Look what I just happen to have here."

She sucked in a breath, shaky with tears that would show in a minute. "You never took it back for a refund."

"Funny, isn't it, how I never did that?"

They stood anxiously on the red carpet of the main hall. The Cross Hall, Trevor called it, staring up at the presidential seal. Reuben thought they were facing the front of the building and Pennsylvania Avenue, but Trevor was quick to point out that Reuben was indicating the South Portico, facing the Washington Monument. Reuben had given up on getting his bearings. At one end of the hall the East Room buzzed with press setting up cameras, and Secret Service, and White House staff. Frank asked Trevor if he was nervous, and Trevor said no, an obvious lie.

The president walked in almost unnoticed, surrounded by Secret Service agents and his press secretary. They just seemed like any other group on first glance. Reuben wondered why he had expected some kind of fanfare.

A moment later the man himself spun off from the group and walked directly to Trevor, looking natural and friendly and unintimidating somehow. He shook Trevor's hand.

"You must be Trevor. Frank treating you okay?"

"Oh, yeah," Trevor said, seemingly unfazed. "Sir. I mean, Mr. President Clinton, sir."

Mr. President Clinton smiled and said Trevor could call him Bill. Trevor turned and shot a look at his mother.

"The press is still setting up, so this'll take a minute. Everybody wants to get this on the news, Trevor."

"Okay by me, Bill, sir."

"So, what have you gotten to see?"

"Everything."

"What did you like best?"

"The cherry blossoms. No, wait. The Vietnam Memorial. That was the best because my mom and Reuben got engaged there."

"Really?" he said, his smiling eyes coming up to take them in. Reuben felt tongue-tied and wished he could handle himself as smoothly and easily as Trevor did. "Well, congratulations."

"Tomorrow's my birthday," Trevor added. "Boy, is it ever gonna be a good one."

"Well, you've just got all kinds of things to celebrate."

"No kidding."

A man arrived at Clinton's elbow. "Mr. President, we're ready to get under way."

Cameras rolled, filling the East Room and filming them with the Cross Hall as backdrop. The president stood beside them, behind a podium, and shook Trevor's hand.

Reuben tried to look natural, but the lights made him want to squint and blink, and between that and his nerves, the whole scene looked and felt surrealistic.

"I'm honored to meet you, Trevor," the president said.

"Yeah, me too," Trevor said. "I mean, I'm honored too. I was so happy when you won the election. I didn't think you had a prayer."

Reuben's jaw tightened. In his peripheral vision he saw Arlene's face go suddenly white.

The president threw his head back and laughed, a big, friendly, genuine laugh. Little lines around his eyes crinkled with amusement. A light stir passed through the press corps.

"Well, Trevor, I guess we're both a good example of what happens when you don't give up on your dreams."

"Yes, sir, Bill, sir. I guess so."

231

By the time Reuben had relaxed enough to be fully present, the visit was over and Frank was driving them back to their hotel.

"That was so incredibly cool," Trevor said.

Reuben felt sorry to have missed it. He consoled himself to know that it would be on the news and his mother would tape it. Maybe he could slow it down and get a better view.

"This has been the best, most incredible day," Trevor said. "You know this means I've only got one more to do."

"One more what?" Arlene asked.

"One more person to help. I got Mrs. Greenberg, and now you two. That only leaves me one more."

"You've done plenty, Trevor. Hasn't he, Reuben?"

"I think you can be proud of what you've already done, Trevor."

"Maybe. But I'll do one more. Somebody else'll need something. Right?"

Reuben and Arlene and Frank all had to agree that it seemed like a reasonably safe bet. Someone always needs something.

CHAPTER TWENTY-SIX

Gordie

He hooked his arm through Harry's as they stepped out into the warm Atascadero night. Gordie turned his head to smile at the restaurant's parking attendant, but he wasn't there.

Then Gordie saw him, off to the left of the awning-covered entryway, his back pressed to the bricks. Holding strangely still. A skinheaded young man stood close, pinning him against the wall. Gordie's knees felt watery and warm at the flash of the blade. Long and mean and curved, bright with use and care.

It occupied his attention until he heard the sound of Harry's breath. The sudden evacuation. And felt Harry's arm pull free as he crumpled away.

Two men stood before Gordie in baggy, low-slung jeans. One tapped a baseball bat against his palm. His military-short hair stuck straight up from

233

his white scalp. One eyebrow had been scarred by a cut and had healed back together mismatched.

"Oops," the man said quietly, his face so close that Gordie could smell tobacco on his breath. "Look what happened to your boyfriend."

Much to Gordie's surprise and relief, he found that the ability to detach had not abandoned him. It would be another beating, like so many before. He would watch it from a distance, and his skin and bones would heal. But he would be elsewhere as it happened, shut down. When you don't care anymore, you deprive them of the joy of hurting you. Hard to hit somebody where they live if there's nobody home.

He closed his eyes, not wanting to see the bat being swung.

It hit him across his soft underbelly, doubling him. A hand around his throat brought him up straight again, and the bat folded him again.

He was going to pass out now, and then it wouldn't matter.

Noises reached his ears through a tunnel. Like the noises in his grandmother's house, where he'd had to sleep in the living room. Sounds that leak through a veil of half sleep, jarring in a distant, disconnected way. Filtering through semiconsciousness.

Just before he sank into it, before muddy gray behind his eyelids turned black, he heard a different sound.

A shouted word. "Hey!"

It could not have come from either of his tormentors. The word started at a high pitch, the voice of a child, then cracked halfway through. The way Gordie's voice had, the way all boys' voices will when they are changing.

The sound of the bat clattering on the pavement. Gordie felt himself turn liquid, boneless. Unsupported by himself or his attackers. He fell softly on what he knew by feel to be the big form of Harry. A comfort. Sparing him from the hard pavement. They would rest here together.

Somehow he remembered feeling Harry's breathing. Perhaps because its presence was something he really needed to feel.

CHAPTER TWENTY-SEVEN

Reuben

A black Lincoln Town Car met them at the air-port and drove them to Atascadero.

Trevor stared out the window, half smiling into the dark. At one point Reuben thought he'd fallen asleep.

Barely seven miles from home, idling at a stop-light, Reuben turned to Arlene, who also seemed to be sleeping. He wanted to say something, maybe whisper it so as not to wake her, but he wasn't sure what it would be. Something about that fact that the amazing trip was over and how that felt.

Before he could open his mouth to speak, he felt night air on his side and heard the traffic sounds suddenly louder. He turned to see that the door on Trevor's side of the car was wide open, and Trevor was gone.

Reuben jumped out into the street.

He saw a small group of figures at the end of the block, outside a building with awnings on the windows. Two men against the building, one on the ground. Two or three standing over the felled man. A baseball bat raised over a head.

And Trevor, running fast in their direction. With a good head start.

Reuben took off after him at a dead sprint.

At the edge of Reuben's vision, the buildings slid by like a dream, a blurred, distorted image through a wide-angle lens. Why couldn't he reach the end of them? He could feel his legs, his heart, opening and straining, yet the distance seemed to stretch out.

Why couldn't he close the gap to the boy?

"Trevor!" he screamed. Screamed. Bellowing, echoing from his lungs, pure panic. Heads turned.

Trevor's head did not.

Reuben's chest ached and burned. How could he be so short of oxygen so fast? He could see Trevor's untucked shirttail flapping out behind him as he ran.

Trevor streaked past the two men pressed against a building. Reuben could see them now, he was almost that close. One of the men wore black pants and a white top, like a waiter or a valet parking attendant. The other wore baggy jeans, his head shaved, and he seemed to have the worker pinned to the building somehow.

The light from the streetlamp glinted off something metal between them, a flash of light in Reuben's eye.

Both men turned their heads as Trevor flew by. The man with the raised bat turned with startled curiosity to watch Trevor's approach.

Without putting on the brakes, Trevor slammed into the man and knocked him down. As he tumbled, he fell against the legs of his accomplice, who also went down. Their second victim crumpled to the sidewalk, untouched, as if an imaginary wind had blown him over. The bat clattered loudly on the sidewalk as Trevor scrambled to his feet.

Reuben had almost drawn level with the men against the building when Trevor turned suddenly, started back in his direction. For what? To head back to Reuben? Or did he think he could knock the last man down?

The skinhead spun away to block Trevor's path. Trevor's impetus carried him forward to that meeting. They came together just a foot or two from the end of Reuben's hand. Reuben could almost have reached out and grabbed the man's jacket, if it hadn't all happened so fast.

Then, just as suddenly, the skinheaded man ran off into the dark. Past his two partners, who scrambled to their feet and sprinted after him, sliding into the night like a river. Just that fast. Someone threw a switch and they were gone.

1994 interview by Chris Chandler, from *Tracking the Movement*

REUBEN: I saw it from so close. But from a funny angle. I was watching the collision from behind. I had no idea what I'd seen. I just remember seeing the man's right elbow come back and then fly forward again. It just looked like he'd punched Trevor in the stomach. Not particularly hard. What I can't figure out is, could I really not see what happened? Or was it just so important to me? You know. Not to see. After they ran off, Trevor was standing there. He looked okay. He had his hands over his stomach. His face was just so open. How do I explain it? He wasn't registering any pain or fear. That I could see.

CHRIS: Breathe. Take your time.

239

REUBEN: I have to tell you this part. What he said. Trevor looked up at my face. Who knows what he saw there? I can't even imagine. I don't even know what I was feeling. I couldn't even tell yet. But some of it must have been right there on my face. He could see it. I could see it on him. It was like looking in a mirror. Then I looked down at Trevor's hands. And then Trevor looked down. It's like he just shifted his eyes down to see where I was looking. And he held his hands out, away from his body, under the light from the streetlamp. He looked so surprised.

CHRIS: Because there was blood, you mean?

REUBEN: He looked up at my face again, and he said, "I'm okay, Reuben. It's okay. Don't worry."

CHRIS: Was he in shock, do you think?

REUBEN: I think he was just trying to comfort me. He didn't want me to be upset.

CHRIS: What do you think motivated him to jump in there? You think he'd just kind of gotten in the habit of trying to help in a big way?

REUBEN: He thought he had to do one more.

CHRIS: We all thought he'd done plenty.

REUBEN: I know. That's what we told him. But he thought Jerry was a failed attempt. He thought he had two down, one to go. So he was on the lookout for somebody who needed something.

CHRIS: If only he'd known about Jerry.

REUBEN: He said he was fine. He told me not to worry.

CHRIS: Did he say anything else?

REUBEN: No. Nothing else.

CHAPTER TWENTY-EIGHT

Chris

He lay under the covers, watching TV.

"Breaking news from Atascadero, California," the anchor announced to open the eleven o'clock news. *This can't be it. Not with the stone face on this newsman. This is not about Trevor.*

"Trevor McKinney, the boy who met with the president of the United States earlier today, has been hospitalized tonight in Atascadero, not far from his family's home. Witnesses say the boy suffered a single stab wound as he tried to intervene in a mugging on the street outside a restaurant. A hospital spokesperson reports that Trevor was admitted in critical condition and is undergoing emergency surgery. No further word on his condition is available at this time."

Chris sat straight up in bed.

"President Clinton tonight expressed deep

concern for Trevor's condition. The president has issued the following statement. Quote: 'It seems unimaginably sad that a boy who was just honored for his good deeds and his dedication to promoting kindness should be targeted in a senseless act of violence. My heart goes out to Trevor and his family, and my family will say a prayer tonight for his speedy recovery. We hope the rest of America will join us in a prayer for Trevor's well-being.'"

The screen filled with the tape of Trevor's earlier meeting with the president. Chris blinked at it, feeling empty.

He rolled out of bed. Looked for the cordless phone. Finally located it in the living room. He punched long-distance information, 805 area code. Asked for a listing for hospitals closest to the Atascadero area.

He hit it on the first try.

The admission desk said yes, Trevor was there. He was in surgery. The woman punched his information up on the computer. "He's listed as critical."

"That's all you can tell me?"

"For the present time, yes. I'm sorry. We're getting a lot of calls about him."

"Where's his mother? Arlene McKinney. She must be there, right?"

"I'm sorry, sir, I couldn't say."

"Could you page her for me?"

A pause, an audible sigh. He heard a click onto hold. He bit the inside of his lip and waited.

Then a voice on the line. "Yeah? Who is this?"

"Arlene? It's Chris, Arlene. Chris Chandler."

"Oh, Chris." Her voice sounded tight and rough.

"What happened, Arlene?"

"Oh, Chris, I don't know. It all happened so fast. He got stabbed. He saw some guys gettin' beat up. He tried to mix in."

"Is he gonna be okay?"

"They won't tell us, Chris." Her voice dissolved into sobs. "He's been in surgery for over two hours. They just won't tell us a thing. They say we'll know when they do. I gotta go, Chris."

The dial tone rang in his ear. He clicked the off button on his phone.

Arlene's front lawn had become a sea of cameras and news teams by the time Chris arrived. He had to park in her driveway behind the Dodge Dart. All the street parking had been taken by television news crew vans.

He cut sideways across her front grass.

"She's not talking to anyone," a female anchor

with stiff, perfect blond hair told him as he stepped onto the front porch.

He rapped hard on the front door. "Arlene? It's me, Chris."

The door peeked open, and Reuben drew him inside by one elbow. Arlene lay on the couch on her side, a glass of water and a box of Kleenex close by.

"I wish they'd go away," she said. "Can you make 'em go away, Chris?"

He sat down on the couch beside her. She patted his hand.

"Everybody cares about this story, Arlene. I've never seen anything like it. I've never seen people mobilize over one story like this."

"It's not a story, Chris. It's happening. And we still don't know if he's gonna be okay."

"I know. I'm sorry. That's just the way I talk."

"I can't talk to all of them. It's too much."

"I know, Arlene. I know. Look, you don't have to talk to anybody. But that Citizen of the Month segment is going to run tomorrow. With an update, of course. If there's anything you want to say, I can get one cameraman in here. That's it. Me and one camera. You don't have to do it. But if there's something you want to tell the public about this, they really want to hear from you."

She sat up, wiped her eyes, and sniffled. "Like what?"

"I don't know. Anything you want to say."

"Well, I could just say there's a vigil tomorrow in front of city hall. We thought maybe even a candlelight march after. You know, if people are interested. If there are people out there who care about Trevor and want him to pull through, they can come and bring a candle. That sort of thing?"

"Yeah. That would be great." Chris felt tears forming, threatening just behind his eyes. "I'll go get a cameraman."

CHAPTER TWENTY-NINE

Arlene

When they arrived home from a morning of sitting helplessly at the hospital, the phone was ringing.

"Let the machine get it," she said.

There were eight other messages showing. Arlene turned the volume all the way down.

She could hear a honking of horns, all the way from the Camino. The intermittent red light of a flashing emergency vehicle slipped by their window.

"Wonder what the heck's going on out there," she said without much genuine curiosity. They had hit surprising traffic jams all the way home.

"An accident, maybe."

"That must be it, yeah."

They tried to get in a little nap before they went back to the hospital, and before that night's vigil for Trevor began.

. . .

Before they left for the vigil, Reuben brought the mail in for the first time in days.

"Here's one addressed to both you and Trevor," he said. "So I guess you can open it if you want."

"Who's it from?"

"A Jerry Busconi."

She just stood a minute, so tired she couldn't even remember if she knew a Jerry Busconi. Then it hit her.

"Read it to me," she said. "Okay?"

Reuben tore open the letter and began to read out loud:

"Dear Trevor and his mom,

I know I'm not your very favorite person. But I'm going to tell you this all the same. First off, I want to say how very sorry I am for that time when you came to visit. Truth is, I was so ashamed I couldn't look either one of you in the eye.

But now I did my time, and I'm living up in San Francisco. Not saying I've got myself all completely together, but I'm still around.

And I paid it forward. Yeah. Me. I really did. I saved somebody's life. That's big, huh? I can't think how to pay it forward any bigger than that. You know how when you get a big bridge like the Golden Gate, somebody might get depressed and want to jump? Well, I kept an eye on the thing for months, and then finally I got a chance to talk some lady out of it. And I know she's still okay, 'cause we have coffee every week. And in case you're wondering, yeah. I'm still living on the street. That's how you keep an eye on a bridge. But don't you see? If I wasn't homeless, I couldn't have done what I did. So even from where I am, I could pay it forward, maybe even do something somebody else can't.

And that's the power of a simple idea.

Well. Just wanted you to know.

Your friend, Jerry Busconi."

As they backed out of the driveway, they noticed both sides of the street solid with parked cars. So close together, pushing so hard for space that they slightly overlapped both sides of the driveway, making it a tight fit to get out. And then, when Reuben had managed to angle straight out between them, he couldn't find a break in traffic. Traffic. On this tiny little residential street.

Arlene got out of the car and personally stopped the procession of cars with her body, giving Reuben a chance to back into the traffic lane.

The VW crawled an inch or two at a time toward the Camino. For the first few minutes they didn't comment or complain.

Arlene glanced at her watch.

"Why is this happening? I mean, today of all days? We're gonna be late if we can't get out of this jam."

Reuben chewed on his lower lip and didn't answer.

It was ten minutes after seven when they hit the Camino, only to find police turning cars away at a roadblock. The main drag appeared closed to traffic. Reuben did not turn where the officer told him to. Instead, he pulled up to the roadblock and rolled down his window. The sun had dipped to a slant behind the officer's head.

Arlene looked straight through the windshield and saw the Camino clogged with pedestrians. Not just the sidewalks, but the street itself. Hundreds, just in this intersection.

"We don't know what's going on," Reuben told the officer, "but we have to get to the vigil at city hall."

"Yeah, that's everybody's problem," he said.

"These people are all here for the vigil?"

"That's right," he said. "Your problem is not unique."

Arlene leaned over Reuben's lap and looked into the officer's face. "I'm Arlene McKinney," she said.

His expression changed. "Right. You are, aren't you? Look, just leave your car here by the barricade and come with me."

Reuben turned off the motor. They stepped out into the sea of bodies and followed the uniformed officer out onto the Camino. The crowd in their immediate vicinity seemed to notice. To recognize. A silence fell, directly surrounding Reuben and Arlene, and rippled out like a wake on water.

A path opened up to allow them through.

They were escorted into the backseat of a black-and-white patrol car. The officer turned on his lights and siren. Through the vehicle's loudspeaker, he asked the crowd to open a traffic lane to allow the family to pass.

Arlene sat straight and rigid, squeezing Reuben's hand, staring forward through the wind-shield, watching the mass of bodies part, watching a ribbon of empty street form ahead of the car.

"This crowd go all the way down to the city hall?" Arlene asked at last, jarring the silence.

"It goes all over town," the officer said. "We got helicopters in from LA. We got mounted police coming in with horse trailers right now. Not that there's been any trouble. There hasn't. We just need more personnel. Local rental company donated some sound equipment. Maybe the people in a four- or five-block radius will hear. Rest'll have to read about it in the paper. Or see it on TV. We got camera crews coming outta our ears."

"How many people do you think we have here?" Reuben asked.

"Most recent estimate stands at twenty thousand. But the freeway's backed up thirty miles. It's a parking lot. They're still coming in."

The patrol car pulled over at the West Mall, and Reuben and Arlene stepped out. She reached for his hand and held it. The officer escorted them through the sea of bodies. A smattering of applause rang in their ears, loudest wherever they happened to walk.

The grassy area overflowed with media equipment. Microphones, cameras, newspeople. They occupied so much space that the nonmedia participants had to squeeze around the edges to allow room for the filming.

It occurred to Arlene that these twenty thousand people might seem like nothing compared to the audience who saw the story reported on the news or in the paper. It was all too much to take in at once.

They reached an elevated makeshift stage, where the sound equipment had been set up. Big, heavy, rock-concert speakers stacked on assembled three-level catwalks, framing city hall. When they stepped onto the stage, the crowd grew quiet. Then a long, steady round of applause broke out.

Chris Chandler slipped up beside her. It felt good to see a familiar face.

"Where did all these people come from, Chris?"

"Well, it just so happens you're asking the right person. I've been conducting interviews in the crowd. The people I've talked to are from"— he flipped open his notepad— "Illinois, Florida, Los Angeles, Las Vegas, Bangladesh, Atascadero, London, San Francisco, Sweden . . ."

"That little television thing I did went outside the country?"

"A hundred and twenty-four countries around the world. Which is, like, nothing compared to the coverage we've got today. Most of these news crews are sending this out live."

Arlene raised her eyes to the crowd, knowing she could see only a tiny percentage. Thousands of people, crowding close to hear. A light dusk had begun to settle. They were late getting started. She looked down at the cameras, saw them looking back. She knew by their red lights that everything, everybody was on. Watching.

She stepped up to the microphone. The crowd waited in silence. She opened her mouth to speak. She felt slightly dizzy. The air, the inside of her head, had taken on the qualities of walking in a dream.

"I'm not too good with words," she said.

Her voice shook and cracked, and the microphone amplified that, ricocheted her tension off the neighboring buildings. The strength of the sound system startled her. The leaves on the oak trees overhead shivered at the sound. All eyes turned up to her in silence.

"I don't even know what I'm doing up here, in front of all these people. I just came here to wish for a recovery for my boy." Tears flowed freely at the sound of those words. She let them. Her voice remained steady and she talked through the moment. The earth seemed to fall out from underneath her. She felt she might pass out. "I'm gonna turn this over to Reuben," she said. "He can talk better than me. I just came here for my boy."

Reuben's arm slid around her shoulder and held tight. *Don't ever let go,* she thought. *Don't you dare ever let go.*

If it wasn't for Reuben, and a hope for Trevor, she'd have nothing left worth holding on to. Except, she thought, maybe this world that had come here to share this moment with her. Maybe that was something after all.

CHAPTER THIRTY

Reuben

Reuben lifted the microphone and pulled it up
to his lips. The light had begun to fade, and artifi-
cial lights glared into his eye from the sea of cameras beneath him. He didn't like lights or cameras
or people staring, but it seemed like a minor concern now.

He opened his mouth to speak, prepared to be
startled by the sound of his own words amplified
into the city dusk.

"The police told me we have more than twenty
thousand people here today. Some have traveled
from outside the country to share this moment
with us. Arlene and I—" His voice cracked slightly
and he stopped. Blinked. Swallowed. "We never
expected anything like this."

Pause. Breathe. He felt light-headed and weak.
What did he want to say? What needed to be said?

Nothing came into his head. What would Trevor want him to say? He opened his mouth and the rest flowed easily.

"The freeway is clogged with thousands more people trying to get here. And I'm told this is going out live. To how many viewers? Millions? How many millions of people am I talking to right now? What made you all care so much? Why is this such a big story? I think I know. I think you know, too. This is our world. Where is the person who can't relate to that? This is our world. It's the only one we've got. And it's gotten so hard to live in. And we care. How can we not care? These are our lives we're talking about. And then a little boy came along, and he decided maybe he could change the whole thing. Make it a decent place to live for everybody. Maybe because he was too young and optimistic and inexperienced to know it couldn't be done. And it looked for a minute like it could work. So, just for a minute, all these people who care enough to be here or to watch this, just for a minute you thought the world might really change. And now Trevor is fighting for his life after a senseless, purposeless act of violence. And that's shaken our faith. So now we wonder. Right? Now we don't know if it can ever get better or not.

"But this is my question to all of you. Why are we here asking the question when we could just as easily be here answering it? Do you want a new world? Because it's not just one little boy anymore. Look at all of us. By the time this has been in all the papers, all the news magazines, been repeated on newscasts all over the world ... the twenty thousand people who made it into the city tonight, that's a drop in the bucket. Twenty million people could hear what I'm about to say.

"So here it is: If Trevor touched your life that much, then maybe you need to pay that forward. In his honor. Twenty million people paying it forward. In a few months that will be sixty million people. And then a hundred and eighty million. In no time at all, that number would be bigger than the population of the world."

Reuben stopped, scratched his head, breathed. Listened for a moment to the echoing silence.

"I know that sounds kind of mind-boggling. But all it really means is that everybody's life would be touched more than once. Three times, six times someone might pay it forward to you. Every month or two, some miraculous act of kindness for everybody. It just keeps getting bigger. Before you could even pay it forward, someone would pay it forward to you again. We'd all lose track after a while. We'd all be scrambling around trying to find people to do good for. We'd never know for sure if we were caught up. It would just keep going around.

"The question I've been asked more than any other . . . every time I'm interviewed for television, every time someone talks to me on the street. They ask, 'How was Trevor's idea received when the class first heard it?' I tell them the truth. I say it was received with an utter lack of respect. It was seen as ridiculous. Because it requires people to work on the honor system, and because they say they'll do all kinds of things, but in the end, people only help themselves. Because they're selfish. They don't care. They don't follow through. Right? People have no honor."

He stopped as if expecting the crowd to answer. Paused on the question they'd all come here to explore. The moment felt heavy in the air.

"Well, then, what are you all doing here? If you don't care. Don't ask me if people will really pay it forward. Tell me. Will you? Will each of you really do it? It's your world. So you decide. I'm getting a little overwrought here. I think I need to drink a glass of water and sit down. We're going to have a candlelight march in a few minutes, when it's dark. So, think about it, and join us then."

The cameras stayed on. Nobody moved. Faces watched him in silence. Applause came up like thunder, spreading down and across the street in all directions, farther than Reuben could see, farther than he knew he could be heard. The whole world, applauding Trevor's idea.

Reuben recognized Chris's face in the candlelight.

Arlene clung tightly to Reuben's hand.

"It's like this," Chris said. "It's not exactly going to be a candlelight march. I mean, everybody brought a candle. But we've got, maybe, thirty-five thousand people here. How you going to march that many people? I mean, from where to where? The city's full. So they're just going to line the street. Like they're doing. And you and Arlene are going to walk. You know? They'll open up a path for you to walk. Right down the middle of the Camino."

"You come with us, Chris," Arlene said suddenly, grabbing at his sleeve.

"No. No way. I don't belong there."

"The heck you don't. Who do you think told all these people about Trevor?"

"I'm not family, though."

"I'm not family by blood, either," Reuben said. "She's right. You come along."

Two uniformed policemen walked on either side of them. Reuben slipped his arm through Arlene's. Their candles flickered in the still night as they moved forward.

The streetlights had not come on. *On purpose?* he wondered. It didn't seem to matter. On every block thousands of candles glowed, lighting up the streets like the full moon that would rise momentarily.

A thin dark ribbon stretched ahead, a path down the middle of the street, left open for them.

Here and there, a hand reached out to lightly touch his shoulder or his sleeve. Round, soft moons of faces shone in the circles of each candle.

A woman reached out and touched Reuben's hand. "I will," she said.

Then the man beside her said the same. "I will."

They passed a mounted policeman on a big bay horse. Sitting still and straight, watching. In one hand he held the reins, in the other a candle. "I will," he said, looking down as they passed.

It spread like a ripple along the route, echoing ten and twenty deep, like the crowd. The simple words followed them along their path, lighting up to their passing. One commitment for every candle.

Everyone said they would.

A NOTE ABOUT THIS EDITION

It took nearly twenty years for me to get serious about becoming a writer. A year or two after that *Pay It Forward* got serious about becoming a book.

It took fourteen years for this edition to follow the original one. Because when I first wrote *Pay It Forward,* not only wasn't it backdated in time, but it was not written for children. Just as I did not imagine that people would really pay it forward, I did not imagine that children would be interested in reading about it. Immediately, it became clear that they were. The book was chosen in 2001 for the American Library Association's Best Books for Young Adults list. And, with that, it crossed over to a high school audience. Younger students remained locked out.

Until now.

This is the same book, just a bit shorter and much more appropriate for the young reader. The characters and the story are the same.

One thing is slightly changed, however. I've done something a little different with the ending. Left it more open. And I know I'll get a lot of questions about it. Children, and probably adults as well, will e-mail me to ask what happened after the last page.

But fiction isn't like that. I don't have a secret key to any parts of the story that aren't on the page. After I stop writing, it's up to you. That's the magic of a story. It's a combination of your imagination and mine. Whatever happens in your mind is just as real as what happens in the mind of the author.

So don't write to me and ask me how it ended. Write to me and tell me how it ended for you.

We'll pool our resources and come up with a memorable story. And maybe . . . just maybe . . . a kinder world.

—Catherine Ryan Hyde

Further Information about
Pay It Forward and the Pay It Forward
Foundation

Do you want to put the ideas in this book into action? Can your school be a Pay It Forward school? Can your students change the world?

The Pay It Forward Foundation thinks they can. And we might be able to help.

The Pay It Forward Foundation was created in 2000 by Catherine Ryan Hyde following the publication of the adult edition of *Pay It Forward*. It was founded on Catherine's vision, and the idea central to the book—that one individual can change the world through simple acts of kindness. Today the foundation's goal is to make paying it forward a daily action and way of life for everyone. We provide resources and information to people who want to join this growing movement and pay it forward.

Catherine Ryan Hyde is helping by donating

a portion of her proceeds from this young readers edition to the Pay It Forward Foundation. What can you do?

To find out more, please visit the foundation website at pifexperience.org and click on the teacher link.

You can also find *Pay It Forward* on Facebook.

A Curriculum Guide to
Pay It Forward: Young Readers Edition

About the Book

Trevor McKinney is an ordinary twelve-year-old boy with a big idea. When his social studies teacher, Reuben St. Clair, assigns an extra-credit project to "Think of an idea for world change and put it into action," Trevor believes he really can change the world. He'll do three enormous favors for three people, and when they ask how they can pay him back, he'll tell them to "pay it forward" to three more people each. He's worked it out on his calculator, and he knows the numbers multiply with incredible speed. What he doesn't know is that everyone might *not* pay it forward according to plan. What the grown-ups around him don't know is that the optimism of a child can be one of the strongest forces on earth.

Prereading Activity

The activity below aligns with the following Common Core State Standards:
(SL.7–8.1)

Brainstorm "acts of kindness" that you or a group of friends could do for someone else. Discuss your list in a small group. Identify one activity to share with the entire class and discuss what you would need to do to complete the project.

Discussion Questions

These discussion questions align with the following Common Core Standards:
(RL.7–8.1, 2, 3, 5)

1. Describe Trevor McKinney's Pay It Forward project. How does he get the idea? Why do others around him think it will fail? Do you believe this kind of project would work? Why or why not?

2. When asked to describe Trevor McKinney, his social studies teacher says, "The thing about Trevor was that he was just like everybody else, except for the part of him that wasn't." How would you characterize Trevor? What accounts for his determination to see his project through? Support your response with events or dialogue from the story.

3. Compare and contrast Trevor's feelings for his father with his feelings for Reuben St. Clair. Describe the relationship between Trevor and Reuben. What bonds the two together?

4. Why does Reuben St. Clair wear an eye patch? How does his disfiguration impact him? How does it affect those around him? Explain how the author reveals the events surrounding Reuben's loss of sight. What does the following passage suggest about Reuben's feelings related to his injury: "But it's not so much *that* they don't ask, but *why* they don't ask, as if I am an unspeakable tragedy, as new and shocking to myself as to them."

5. Analyze how the characters Arlene McKinney and Reuben St. Clair change over the course of the story. Both characters have conflicting emotions. Describe the internal conflict with which each character struggles. How does their relationship develop? What role does Trevor play in their relationship?

6. How is Trevor impacted by his father's return? How is Arlene? Reuben? Is Ricky a likeable person? Explain. How does Ricky serve to advance the plot?

7. How does Trevor meet Jerry Busconi and why does Trevor invite him into his house? Arlene becomes upset with Trevor when she learns that Jerry showers in their house. Is her frustration warranted? Explain.

8. What act of kindness does Trevor do for Mrs. Greenberg and how does she pay it forward? Why is her son, Richard, disappointed in her behavior? Do you agree with the son? Why or why not?

9. Why does Arlene take Trevor to visit Jerry in prison? What happens to prevent them from seeing Jerry? How are Arlene's and Trevor's reactions different when they learn they will not see Jerry? Why do you think Jerry refuses to see them?

10. Why does Roger Meagan call Chris Chandler? How does Chris "track the movement"? What does he discover about people along the way? How does Chris find Trevor? Is Trevor aware of the impact of his project? Explain.

11. Describe Trevor's trip to Washington, DC. Compare this scene with the one following it in which Trevor is stabbed when he intervenes in a mugging. How do the two scenes increase the emotional intensity of the story's ending? Why does Trevor intervene in the mugging?

12. Identify two themes and analyze how they develop over the course of the story. Discuss how these two themes build on and support each other as the story progresses.

13. Analyze the point of view the author uses to tell the story. Why does the author not use first-person point of view from Trevor's perspective? Chris Chandler is an investigative reporter. What role does he play in telling the story? How does the author use his character to structure the story?

14. Discuss how the author structures the story. In your discussion, take into account how the writings of the investigative reporter Chris Chandler and Trevor's diary entries progress the plot.

15. The author changed the ending of this version of *Pay It Forward*. She writes, "One thing is slightly changed, however. I've done something a little different with the ending. Left it more open. And I know I'll get a lot of questions about it. Children, and probably adults as well, will e-mail me to ask me what happened after the last page." Do you like how the story ends? Why or why not? What possibilities can you imagine? Why do you think the author made this change? Hint: In the original version, the reader clearly knows Trevor dies.

Activities

These activities align with the following Common Core State Standards:
(SL.7–8.1) (W.7–8.1, 2, 7)

1. Revisit the list you brainstormed in the prereading activity for this novel and expand on ideas you and/or your friends could do to pay it forward. Discuss these ideas in a small group. Choose one idea from your group discussion and work with a family and/or friend to develop a plan for implementing the idea.

2. Trevor had several different ideas of how to pay it forward. Some of them were good ideas. Others put him in danger, and if an adult had known, they would have told Trevor his plans were not good ones. Write about what you would do if you decided to pay it forward. How would you avoid some of Trevor's mistakes and be sure that your plans were safe?

3. Write a letter to Trevor and explain one of the following: a) why you think he is a hero or b) why you think he is not. You might choose instead to write the letter to Arlene, his mother, or to his teacher Reuben.

4. Write an essay about a topic that bothers you most about the world and explain what people could do to make the situation better. Support your essay with information you gather from the Internet. Remember to cite any sources appropriately.

5. Discuss in a small group things you could do to make your school a more inviting place for students, faculty, and staff. In your discussion consider the following: a) how to make new students feel more welcome; b) how to address bullying behaviors; c) how to make students, faculty, and staff feel more valued. Put one action step in place, either as a group or as an individual.

6. Research charities and other organizations in your community for which you can volunteer. Make a list of these organizations and the volunteer work students can do for the organization. Publish these organizations and the volunteer activities in a brochure and/or on a class website.

7. Some schools build curricula around service-learning projects—projects that give to the community but that are also tied to the class curriculum. Work with your teachers to identify service-learning projects that are tied to your future studies. You might talk with your teachers about an interdisciplinary project that spans several classes.

Guide written by Pam B. Cole, Professor of English Education & Literacy, Kennesaw State University, Kennesaw, GA

This guide, written in alignment with the Common Core Standards (www.corestandards.org), has been provided by Simon & Schuster for classroom, library, and reading group use. It may be reproduced in its entirety or excerpted for these purposes.